THE MUMMY CASE

THE HARDY BOYS™ MYSTERY STORIES

THE MUMMY CASE

Franklin W. Dixon

**Illustrated by
Leslie Morrill**

WANDERER BOOKS
Published by Simon & Schuster, New York

Manufactured in the United States of America
10 9 8 7 6 5 4 3 2 1

WANDERER and colophon are trademarks
of Simon & Schuster

Library of Congress Cataloging in Publication Data

Dixon, Franklin W
The mummy case.

(His Hardy boys mystery stories; 63)
SUMMARY: Called in to investigate the theft of some
statuettes stolen from the Egyptian Museum in New York,
the Hardy brothers become involved in a deepening mystery
which includes the possible overthrow of another
country's government.
[1. Mystery and detective stories]   I. Morrill,
Leslie H.   II. Title.
PZ7.D644Ms   [Fic]   80-12881
ISBN 0-671-41116-0
ISBN 0-671-41111-X (pbk.)

Contents

1

Museum Mystery

Frank Hardy tossed a baseball into the air, brought his bat around in a flashing arc, and hit a line drive that his brother Joe caught with a quick backhand stab.

Joe grinned. "Not bad, eh? Just throw me anything and I'll get it!"

"Pure luck!" Frank retorted. "That one had base hit written all over it."

The boys were practicing in their back yard for their high-school team's big game with Bayport's arch rival, Greenpoint. Just then their Aunt Gertrude poked her head out of the kitchen door.

"Frank and Joe! You're wanted on the phone."

"Who is it, Aunt Gertrude?" Frank asked.

"Your father. Come quickly. He's calling long-distance." Gertrude Hardy, who had been living with her brother's family for quite some time, waved impatiently. She had a habit of disguising her fondness for her nephews behind a crisp, no-nonsense manner.

Frank and Joe ran into the house. Frank picked up the hall phone while his brother went to get the extension in his father's study. "Hi, Dad," the dark-haired, eighteen-year-old boy said. "What's up?"

"A new case," Mr. Hardy replied. "Are you both there?"

"Yes," Joe spoke into the receiver. "Go ahead."

Fenton Hardy, the famous private detective, sounded serious. "Listen carefully. I'm at the United Nations in New York, working on an assignment for one of its members. I've learned about a plot to overthrow that nation's government. That's all I can say, because it's highly confidential. A leak might trigger an international crisis, and Uncle Sam would be right in the middle of it!"

"What can we do to help?" Joe inquired excitedly.

"Nothing on this case," Mr. Hardy replied. "But there's something else I'd like you to handle for me. Go to New York tomorrow morning and see Curator Henry Wilcox at the Egyptian Museum. Some

2

statuettes were stolen from the collection. Wilcox wanted me to look into it but I can't because of this UN investigation."

"Sure, Dad," Frank said. "We'll be glad to."

"If you need help, call Sam Radley," his father added. Radley was one of his top operatives who had assisted the Hardys on many of their assignments.

Mr. Hardy now asked to speak to the boys' mother, and Frank and Joe returned to the yard. They resumed their baseball practice and Joe hit a couple of grounders. "We've worked on a lot of thefts," the blond, seventeen-year-old amateur detective said, "but we've never chased ancient Egyptian statuettes before!"

Frank grinned. "I hope we catch them. With Dad busy on another case, I'd hate to let him down."

Aunt Gertrude had come into the yard to hang up clothes. "Ancient Egyptians, eh?" she sniffed. "Next thing I know you'll be playing baseball with a mummy!"

"If a mummy can hit, we'll put him on the team," Joe declared.

Next morning, the Hardy boys had an early breakfast, then set off on the long drive to New York City. When they reached the museum, they parked their yellow sports sedan in the garage underneath the building and went upstairs. They identified themselves to one of the staff members and asked to speak to Mr. Wilcox. After a brief conversation on his intercom, the man told them to go to the curator's office. "Take the main stairs," he directed, "then go down the hall past the Weapons Room. Mr. Wilcox's office is at the very end."

Frank and Joe walked between two replicas of an Egyptian sphinx flanking the staircase, reached the next floor, and went down the hall. As they passed the Weapons Room, they saw an arsenal of ancient arms. Swords, bows, spears, and daggers hung on the walls and a chariot stood in the middle of the room.

"There's enough military hardware in there to start a war," Frank commented with a grin, then he knocked on the curator's door. Wilcox opened it. He was a tall man wearing rumpled clothing and horn-rimmed glasses. The boys recognized him at once. A famous archeologist, he had been photographed by journalists and television crews at digs in Egypt.

"You must be the Hardy boys," Wilcox said as he shook hands with the visitors. "Your father told me you'd come. I'm glad you can take this case."

He led the young detectives into his office, motioning for them to sit down. Then he settled himself in a swivel chair behind his large desk.

"Tell us about the robbery," Joe began. "All we know is that some statuettes are missing."

4

"The pieces disappeared one night from the Statuary Room," Wilcox declared. "Five small golden statuettes of the ancient pharaohs." He handed the boys a number of photographs. "Here they are. It happened last week."

"Does the museum have an alarm system?" Frank inquired.

The curator nodded. "But it didn't go off!"

"Perhaps it was an inside job," Frank conjectured. "The thief could be someone who works here and knows how the alarm functions."

Wilcox nodded. "The police arrived at the same conclusion. That's why I had the system changed immediately. Now even the guards don't know how it operates. I was advised to keep it a secret. If the thief is one of my staff and makes another attempt, he'll trigger the alarm."

"The police are working on the case?" Joe asked.

"Yes. But I felt it would be good for an outsider or two to help. You can mingle with the staff more easily and might find out something the police didn't. People are wary when they talk to the authorities. They might speak more freely to you."

"We'll be glad to do all we can," Frank said.

"Good. As for the robbery, I'll have the guard describe it to you."

Wilcox snapped on his intercom. "Have Ahmed Ali report to my office," he said.

Ali was a small, dark Egyptian with black eyes

5

and a nervous manner. "I was on duty that night," he testified. "I saw and heard nothing. The statuettes were there when I checked the room early in the evening. Next morning, they were gone!"

"Where were you during the rest of the night?" Frank inquired.

"Checking the other rooms," the Egyptian said defensively. "I—"

"It wasn't his fault," Wilcox put in. "His partner on guard duty became sick and had to go home. It takes two men to patrol the entire museum, but Ali had to do it alone that night."

After a few more inconclusive answers, the man left.

"He wasn't much help," Frank said. "But I suppose he's our one and only suspect so far, simply because he was *here* at the time of the theft."

"The police questioned Ali and found nothing," Wilcox declared. "Also, we've never had any reason to mistrust Ali. He's—"

A loud clanging reverberated through the building and interrupted the curator's sentence. On a control board near his phone, a red light began to flash.

Wilcox stared at it in surprise. "The alarm!" he exclaimed. "Somebody's in the Weapons Room!"

He jumped up from his chair and headed for the door with the Hardys close behind him. All three hurried to the Weapons Room.

Ali was standing near the wall, holding an Egyptian dagger in his hand! The sharp blade gleamed as he stood perfectly still, an astonished expression on his face.

"What are you doing?" Wilcox demanded sternly.

The guard slowly lowered the dagger. "It was loose on the wall, so I took it down to straighten the clamp. I didn't realize that it was enough to set off the burglar alarm. It never went off before."

"Well, it does now. See that things are not removed from their displays in the future."

"I will," Ali murmured as he put the dagger back on the wall. Then he quickly went out of the Weapons Room.

Joe examined the clasp holding the dagger. "I don't see anything wrong with it," he declared.

"Neither do I," Frank agreed. "I think Ali was fooling with the dagger for his own purposes. I wonder if he was trying to steal it? Though that would be pretty stupid with us here!"

Wilcox agreed, nodding his head. "Well, let's go back to my office. I have my two assistant curators coming in, William Colden and Najeeb Salim, and I'd like you to speak to them."

After Wilcox was seated behind his desk again, he turned off the burglar alarm, then inquired over the intercom about Colden and Salim. He was told that the two men had not yet returned from the Metropolitan Museum of Art, where they had been

inspecting a new shipment of Egyptian artifacts.

"While we're waiting," Wilcox suggested, "I'll show you something that might interest you."

"What's that?" Joe asked.

"The mummy of an unknown Egyptian pharaoh who died about three thousand years ago. It was stolen!"

2

The Pharaoh's Warning

"Stolen!" Joe gasped. "Another robbery here at the museum?"

"No," Mr. Wilcox replied. "This mummy was taken out of Egypt by an unscrupulous archeologist many years ago. We purchased it in good faith. However, when Najeeb Salim joined our staff, he proved to me that the mummy really belongs to his country. So, we're preparing to send it back. Salim will accompany it and make the official presentation in Cairo. He'll sail the day after tomorrow aboard the freighter *Admiral Halsey*.

"Mr. Colden contends that a ship is the safest way of transport," Wilcox continued. "He's in charge of the mummies in the museum, so I'm taking his advice. Would you like to see the mummy?"

Frank and Joe agreed enthusiastically, and Wilcox took them through the hall to an elevator that carried them into the basement.

In one corner, a specialist was fitting bits of broken pottery together. Two men were measuring a small sphinx, whose damaged head lay beside it, while a woman was sorting out a box full of jewelry.

Wilcox led the way to the opposite side of the room near the stairs. Here, all by itself, the Hardys saw an ornate Egyptian case or sarcophagus. The lid bore the likeness of the pharaoh who had been buried in it. The headdress extended down to his shoulders, meeting a gown that reached to his feet. The face was shown in repose, its features carefully painted in brilliant colors. The chin terminated in a long, narrow beard, and the arms were crossed over the chest with one hand holding a scepter, the other a flail.

"I suppose you know the meaning of the scepter and the flail?" the curator asked.

"We've both studied Egyptian history in high school," Frank said. "The scepter is a symbol of the pharaoh's right to rule."

"And the flail," Joe added, "means he had a right to knock anybody on the head who didn't obey."

Wilcox smiled. "You're good students as well as good detectives. Now let's open the case."

11

With the curator's help, Frank and Joe lifted the lid and placed it carefully on the floor.

"Meet our mummy," Mr. Wilcox said. "I'm sorry I can't introduce him by name, but we still haven't figured out who he was."

An eerie feeling penetrated the Hardys as they gazed down at the pharaoh who had been dead for three thousand years. He was wrapped from head to foot in linen cloth, with the features of his face painted on the bandages. Through holes in the linen, two artificial black eyes were staring at the boys.

"He—he almost looks alive!" Joe stammered. "As if he were about to say something to us!"

"That's what the ancient Egyptians intended," Mr. Wilcox replied. "They wanted the embalmed mummy to be as lifelike as possible for its journey to the next world."

"Embalmed?" Frank asked. "The pharaoh was embalmed?"

"That's correct," the curator declared. "It was a complicated process that's still somewhat of a mystery. But we do know that most of the internal organs were removed, then the body was put in a jar of salted water. Sometimes preservatives were used, such as resin and natron."

"And then?" Joe asked. "I mean, you can't just salt a guy in a jar and expect he'll last forever!"

Wilcox laughed. "Of course not. The ancient Egyptians filled the body with other chemicals, wrapped it tightly, and put it in its case. The burial site was the Valley of the Kings."

"That's up the Nile near Luxor where they buried the pharaohs in the cliffs, isn't it?" Frank said.

"That's right. They covered the tombs to keep them from being found. But grave robbers got into all of them, except the one of King Tutankhamen."

Joe smiled. "We saw the exhibition of King Tut's treasures," he said. "It was fantastic how well everything was preserved."

Frank noticed hieroglyphics on the case above the mummy's head. "Do you know what these mean, Mr. Wilcox?"

"It's the pharaoh's curse."

Frank felt a cold chill run up and down his spine. He stared at the mummy, mesmerized for a moment, then shook himself out of his trance. "What curse? What's this guy saying to us?"

"I'll translate it into verse," the curator replied. "It goes something like this:

Cursed is he
Who touches me;
He soon shall die
Whose face I spy."

Joe shuddered. "It gives me the creeps!"

13

"The ancient Egyptians wrote this type of warning because they thought it would protect the mummy," Wilcox went on. "Unfortunately, it didn't help much."

"It worked in the case of King Tut," Joe pointed out. "If I remember correctly, Lord Carnarvon, the British aristocrat who financed the search, died shortly afterward."

"That's right," Frank added. "He didn't even see the mummy of Tutankhamen. It was found later."

"On the other hand," Wilcox said, "Howard Carter, who directed the excavation, lived to a ripe old age!"

Joe grinned. "If King Tut put the whammy on anybody, it should have been Carter. The pharaoh knocked off the wrong man!"

"That's about it," Wilcox agreed. "But don't underestimate the power of the pharaoh's warning. Many people still believe in it."

Frank and Joe replaced the lid on the mummy's coffin, then they all went back to the curator's office. Two men were waiting for them. One, William Colden, was short, rotund, and had a friendly smile. The other, Najeeb Salim, was a tall, thin man with a dark complexion and a solemn expression on his face. Although he wore Western dress, he was unmistakably Egyptian.

"We were caught in traffic," Colden apologized

after the introductions had been made. "That's why we're late."

Wilcox nodded. "I showed Frank and Joe the mummy in the meantime. They're here to investigate the theft of the golden statuettes."

Salim glowered at the Hardys. "And have you discovered the culprit?"

"So far we haven't much to go on," Frank replied, "except for maybe Ahmed Ali and the dagger." He described the event in the Weapons Room after the alarm had gone off. "Ali could have stolen the statuettes," he added. "He knew about the alarm system the museum used to have, and he was on guard that night."

Wilcox got to his feet. "I'd like to stay longer," he said, "but I have to catch a plane to Chicago for a conference of archeologists. In fact, I'm the main speaker. You boys know what you have to do, so I'll leave the investigation to you."

"What about the mummy?" Colden asked.

"You and Najeeb are in charge," Wilcox replied. "See that the case is prepared for shipment to Cairo and cooperate with Frank and Joe in the matter of the stolen statuettes."

Wilcox left, and Colden excused himself to make a phone call. Najeeb Salim stood up and paced around the room. "Perhaps we should have Ali arrested at once!" he proposed.

15

"We can't," Frank said. "There's no real evidence against him. Even though we saw him holding the dagger, we don't know what he intended to do with it."

"Then we should dismiss him! Why give him another chance to steal?"

The Egyptian's vehemence began to arouse Frank's suspicion. "Maybe Salim's involved in this and is looking for a scapegoat," he thought.

The same idea occurred to Joe, who made a mental note to keep an eye on Salim. Just then Colden returned from his office. "I talked to Cairo," he announced. "They're ready for you and the mummy, Najeeb. How's the investigation coming along?" he asked Frank and Joe.

Frank shrugged. "Ali is our prime suspect so far, but we don't have any proof. What do *you* think, Mr. Colden?"

"I think we should have a cup of coffee," the assistant curator replied, "and go over the events point by point. I'll call the kitchen. Will you boys join us?"

"I'd prefer a soda," Frank said. "There's a machine at the end of the hall. How about you, Joe?"

"Soda's fine."

Frank went out and came back with two colas. He handed one to Joe just as the woman who ran the museum's kitchen arrived in the office. She was an

16

attractive blonde in her late twenties whose some-what sharp features softened for a moment as she smiled at the boys.

"I'm Norma Jones," she said. "If you want any-thing from the galley, just say the word."

Colden settled himself on the sofa with Salim be-side him and the Hardys occupied the chairs in front of the desk. Norma Jones left and closed the door behind her.

"The police interrogated the staff," Colden be-gan, "but no one could shed any light on the mat-ter."

"I suppose they searched the premises for clues?" Joe inquired.

"They did," Salim replied. "It took hours since there was no sign of breaking and entering. But—" Suddenly a strange look came over him. His pupils dilated, and his breath came in short gasps. He shuddered and ran his fingers around his collar in an effort to loosen it.

"Mr. Salim," Frank exclaimed, "are you okay?"

There was no reply. Instead, the Egyptian jerked to his feet and lunged toward the young detective. His fingers reached for Frank's throat in a convul-sive grip! The chair went over backward, and the pair landed on the carpet. Savagely, Salim tried to strangle Frank Hardy!

3

Mummy Powder

Joe leaped to his brother's aid, but Frank had already managed to break Salim's grip. Pushing the Egyptian aside, he scrambled clear. Salim jerked to his feet again. For a moment he swayed there and the boy braced for another violent attack. However, Salim suddenly collapsed onto the carpet, rolled over, and lay motionless!

"Wow!" Joe exclaimed. "What got into him?"

Frank pointed at Colden. "Something's wrong with both of them!"

Colden was leaning back on the sofa. His eyes were closed, and he gasped loudly. Joe shook him, and gradually the man stopped gasping. Opening his eyes, he said, "W-what happened?"

"You tell us!" Joe responded.

"I must have passed out," Colden murmured.

Frank bent over Salim and slapped his face a few times. The Egyptian let out a low moan, then slowly opened his eyes. He looked pale. "What are you doing?" he whispered.

"Trying to get you back to reality," Frank replied. "You almost strangled me, then you collapsed on the floor!"

"What!" Salim stared at the boy in utter disbelief. "But—but I don't remember any of this!"

Joe had examined the coffee cups. Both were still half-filled. "Frank!" he called out, "there's something in here. A powder. I can see it on the rim of one cup!"

Salim gasped. "Someone tried to poison me!"

"Not only you, both of us!" Colden added.

"Oh, what a terrible, terrible thing!" Salim struggled to his feet with Frank's help, then sat down on the sofa again. "May I see the cup?"

Joe handed it to him. "Right here," he said and pointed to minute specks of gray powder. "Do you have any idea what this is?"

Salim stared at it for a few moments. "It looks like mummy powder."

"What's that?"

"In my country," Salim explained, "mummies were ground up in the days gone by. Mummy pow-

19

der was supposed to cure a lot of ailments. I have some here in the museum to display in my lectures on the mummies of Egypt."

He gave the cup to Colden. "What do you think?"

"Looks like mummy powder all right," his colleague confirmed.

"But could it have such an effect on you?" Joe asked. "It doesn't sound like a poison."

Salim shook his head. "It's quite harmless. But perhaps there's something else in our cups!"

"Let's go up to the lab and ask for an analysis of the coffee," William Colden suggested.

"Good idea," Frank said. "Do you feel well enough to come with us, Mr. Salim?"

"I'd rather stay here and rest," the Egyptian said with a weak smile. "If you don't mind."

"Of course not. Are you okay, Mr. Colden?"

"Yes. I feel a bit light-headed, but I'll show you where the lab is."

The boys followed the assistant curator up one flight to the large museum laboratory. A red-haired man in a white lab coat pushed his glasses up on his forehead and smiled when they entered. "What can I do for you?"

Joe placed the two cups on a bench. "Tell us what's in here."

The chemist peered into the cups. "Coffee," he said.

"We know. But it was laced with something that made both Mr. Colden and Mr. Salim pass out."

"Not only that," Frank added, "Mr. Salim became aggressive before losing consciousness. Does that suggest anything to you?"

The chemist whistled. "It sounds like heliomin. It's a brand-new chemical compound we use in our work. If ingested, it can cause drastic personality changes, and the victim may go berserk. I've warned everyone about that and told the staff to be careful with the stuff."

"Does it have any lasting effects?" Frank asked worriedly, thinking about Najeeb Salim.

"Not that I know of. But let me test the coffee first to be sure it's heliomin." The chemist took the two cups and examined them closely. "Seems there's a little mummy powder in here, too."

Colden nodded. "The culprit must have added it as the final touch!" he said ironically.

The chemist took some coffee from one of the cups with an eyedropper and squeezed it into a test tube. Drawing a light-colored liquid from a jar, he allowed one drop to fall into the tube. The mixture became colorless. The same happened when the second cup was tested.

"It's heliomin all right," he confirmed. "Where on earth did you get that coffee?"

"From the kitchen," Colden replied.

The chemist was greatly alarmed. "This is a very serious matter! You have to report it—"

"I'll take care of it, Jim," Colden interrupted. "We don't want to cause any panic. Besides, I've a feeling it's related to the thefts that took place a week ago. Frank and Joe Hardy here are investigating the case. So I'd appreciate it if you'd keep the whole thing under your hat for the time being."

"If you say so," the chemist agreed reluctantly. "But I hope you realize how serious this is!"

"I certainly do!" Colden said sharply. "Remember, I got a dose of this stuff!" He turned to the boys. "Come on, let's go down to the kitchen."

The trio went back to the elevator and rode to the first floor. They found Norma Jones in a small galley where she prepared food and drink for the museum staff. Frank asked her where the coffee had come from that she had served to Colden and Najeeb Salim.

She pointed to a large urn bubbling on the counter. "From there, as always. Any complaints?"

"Yes," Frank said. "The coffee was laced with heliomin and mummy powder. Knocked out Mr. Colden and Mr. Salim. Do you know anything about it?"

Norma Jones went ashen white. "Why—why of course not! Why are you asking me?"

"You made the coffee."

"Sure, but I didn't put anything in it. Not even cream and sugar!"

"Were you in the kitchen all the time?" Joe asked.

"Of course not. I've other work to do, you know. I clean certain areas of the museum and I'm in charge of supplies. Besides, I served coffee from that pot to other people, and no one has complained!"

She turned to Colden in great agitation. "Why are you accusing me? I don't even know what heliomin is!"

"Calm down, Norma," the assistant curator said gently. "No one's accusing you. We're just trying to find out what happened. Tell me, did you bring the cups right up after you poured them?"

Norma shook her head. "No. I had two orders at the same time. One cup for Mr. Molina in the Accounting Department, and two for you. I served Mr. Molina first because he's right next door."

"Then somebody could have sneaked in here and drugged the coffee for Mr. Salim and myself!" Colden declared.

"That's what must have happened," Norma agreed. "You do believe me, don't you, Mr. Colden?"

"Of course, Norma. We'll investigate the matter

at once, but if word leaks out it might hamper our search for the culprit. So please keep quiet about the incident, will you?"

"Sure," Norma said. "I want you to find out that I had nothing to do with it!"

The assistant curator and the Hardys left the kitchen and returned to Mr. Wilcox's office. On the way, they discussed the frightening incident.

"If someone put heliomin and the mummy powder into the cups while Norma was out of the kitchen, how come she didn't notice the powder when she brought the coffee upstairs?" Joe said. "*We* saw it!"

"After you looked closely," Colden reminded him. "She had no reason to do that."

Najeeb Salim was still resting on the couch when the trio entered. He was pale and complained about chest pains.

"We'll take you to the doctor," Frank volunteered.

The Egyptian nodded gratefully. "I have a heart ailment, and this seems to have aggravated it," he said.

Joe turned to Colden. "Would you like to come along, too?"

Colden shook his head. "I feel all right now. You go ahead and I'll continue with my preparations for the mummy's departure."

24

The Hardys drove Salim to his doctor. After being examined, the assistant curator came into the waiting room, greatly upset.

"The doctor wants me to go to the hospital for a few days," he said. "He thinks the drug might have affected my heart condition. Do you realize what this means? I won't be able to go to Egypt and deliver the mummy!"

Joe put a hand on his arm. "Mr. Salim, your health is more important. We'll take you right to the hospital and then report to Mr. Colden. He'll find someone else to escort the coffin to Egypt."

Salim shrugged. "You're right. I have no choice. Thanks for being so helpful. Would you mind stopping off at my house so I can pick up a few things?"

"Of course not," Frank said.

It took less than an hour to deliver the assistant curator to the hospital. When he was signed in, and the boys were about to leave, Frank suddenly stopped short. "I think we should call Mr. Wilcox at the airport," he said. "If we're lucky, we'll still catch him."

They found a public telephone booth and had the curator paged. His plane had been delayed, and he was still in the terminal. He was disturbed about the events at the museum and worried about Salim's illness.

"If I didn't have this speaking engagement I'd

25

come right back," he said. "As for Najeeb, of course he can't travel under the circumstances. But I can't spare Colden either. He's in charge while Mr. Salim and I are away. Say, would you boys be willing to make the voyage in Najeeb's place? The museum will reimburse you for all your expenses."

"I suppose we could go," Frank replied. "We'll have to check with our father. What about the theft investigation?"

"We'll have to find someone else," Wilcox said.

"I have an idea," Frank put in. "Sam Radley, our father's operative, might be able to help out. Do you want us to give him a call?"

"That would be fine. Please arrange everything with Mr. Colden." The curator hung up.

Frank and Joe returned to the museum and discussed their plans with William Colden. He was relieved to hear that the mummy transport could proceed as planned and promised to cooperate with Sam Radley on the theft investigation. Luckily Radley could be reached and agreed to report to the museum the following morning.

By now most of the staff had already left because it was well after closing time. Colden looked worn and tired. "I wonder if you could do me a favor before returning to Bayport," he asked.

"Sure," Frank said. "What is it?"

"I don't want to leave the mummy unguarded

tonight. I was going to stay here, but I feel pretty woozy. Do you think you could take over for me?"

"No problem," Frank stated. "We'll be glad to stay till tomorrow."

"Where do we sleep?" Joe asked.

"Right next to the mummy. We'll set up a couple of cots for you."

After dinner in a nearby restaurant, the assistant curator led the way to the elevator, down to the basement, and to the mummy case. A single light bulb in the ceiling threw a lurid glare over the figure of the pharaoh on the lid, accentuating the stare of the black eyes.

The curator opened the coffin. "Everything's all right," he declared. "Tomorrow we fasten the case, wrap it in protective cloth, and have it sealed in a crate."

A thought struck Joe. "Mr. Colden, when Sam Radley takes over our investigation tomorrow, ask him to keep an eye on Ahmed Ali. I still think he's involved in the thefts."

"Oh, I forgot to tell you. That won't be possible."

"Why not?"

"Ali seems to have disappeared!"

4

The Weird Intruder

"What!" Frank and Joe were flabbergasted.

"You boys were right in suspecting Ali," Colden went on. "He left the museum early this afternoon, and when I called his boardinghouse, his landlady told me he had paid her and taken off without leaving a forwarding address."

"Did you inform the police?" Frank asked.

"Yes, I did," Colden replied. "They're looking for him now."

The assistant curator pulled a couple of cots from a shelf, and the Hardys helped him set them up on either side of the mummy case. Then he tossed some blankets at them. "It isn't the Ritz, but it's the best we can do under the circumstances," he apologized.

"We'll be all right," Frank assured him.

"Good. Then I'll turn out all the lights and lock the door. And thanks for doing me the favor."

Colden disappeared up the stairs. A moment later the Hardys heard the front door slam. Then silence descended over the museum.

Frank and Joe sat down on the cots with the mummy in between.

"What do you suppose our roommate's thinking?" Joe asked.

Frank stretched. "I don't know and I don't care. I'm tired." He lay back on the cot with his hands behind his head.

"This is a creepy place," Joe complained.

"Well, put the light out and you'll forget all about it. I just hope the pharaoh doesn't snore."

"Or walk in his sleep," Joe grumbled. The darkness seemed to close in on him. On the floor above, the idols of ancient Egypt kept their vigil, as they had for centuries on the banks of the Nile in the temples of gods. The mummy lay in its case next to the Hardys, and Joe could imagine the artificial eyes staring upward. The basement stairs creaked, and the boy raised his head to listen. But silence fell again. Joe lay back and soon was sound asleep.

A hand closing on his shoulder brought him awake with a start. A light shone on him and he raised a hand to shield his eyes. Then a face pushed forward toward his.

29

It was a mummy! Two black eyes glared at Joe through the bandages swathing the head. Its body was clothed in the long gown of an Egyptian pharaoh, and in its hand it held a Nile cobra with upraised head, spreading hood, and bared fangs!

The figure laughed in a high pitch that made Joe's flesh crawl. Then the light went out and the boy heard footsteps ascending the stairs. He jumped out of his cot in a wide arc to avoid the snake if it was there, shouted a warning to Frank, and followed the mummy as quickly as he could in the darkness.

He rushed through the door at the top of the stairs and found himself in the museum's main room. It was bright with moonlight slanting through the windows. The intruder tried to hide behind a tall stone statue of Osiris, the Egyptian god of the underworld. But when Joe spotted him, he made a dash for the front door.

Joe chased him across the room, past cases laden with relics of ancient Egypt, and closed the gap just as they reached the entrance. Suddenly the figure whirled around and clubbed Joe on the side of the head! With a gasp, the young detective tumbled to the floor and blacked out!

Joe regained consciousness to find the front door open and the gruesome intruder gone. In the moonlight he saw splinters of glass and a dented flashlight lying next to him.

31

"That's what he hit me with!" the boy thought angrily, rubbing the side of his head. "And that's the light he used downstairs."

Joe got to his feet, locked the front door, and returned to the basement. Frank had put on the light and was examining a serpent of ancient Egypt. He held it up for Joe to see.

"I found this in front of your bed!" he said. "It's made of polished wood."

"A guy came in here dressed like a mummy. He was holding it," Joe explained. "It looked so real in the glow of his flashlight I was scared to death."

Frank chuckled.

"It wasn't funny!" Joe exploded.

"I know. But even a mummy wouldn't handle a live cobra, Joe!"

"Of course not. But I didn't have time to think of that. What do you make of the whole thing?"

"First tell me exactly what happened," Frank urged.

"The guy put a hand on my shoulder and shone his light into my face."

"Then I guess he wasn't after our mummy, which, incidentally, I checked on. The intruder's purpose must have been to scare us. Perhaps he doesn't want us to go to Egypt."

Joe nodded. He was examining the bump on his

head with his fingertips and groaned. "Maybe the curse is working!" he said ominously.

Frank grimaced. "Let's go back to sleep!"

In the morning, the boys reported the incident to William Colden, who arrived at the museum much refreshed. He had no idea who the intruder could have been, and the two guards had heard nothing.

"Whoever it was, he must have had a key to the door," Joe pointed out. "Also, he knew how to avoid the alarm system. It could have been Ahmed Ali!"

Colden went to Mr. Wilcox's office, and returned a few seconds later greatly disturbed. "The alarm was off!" he cried out. "And I checked last night just before I went home to make sure it was working!"

Just then Sam Radley arrived. He was younger than Mr. Hardy, with sandy hair and a friendly smile on his face.

"We're so glad you're here," Frank greeted him and introduced him to the assistant curator. "We have to leave to prepare for our trip, but Mr. Colden will give you all the details of the case."

"Run along, boys," Radley said cheerfully. "I promise to find the thieves while you're on vacation with your mummy!"

The Hardys drove back to Bayport and informed their mother and Aunt Gertrude of their impending trip.

"You're headed for trouble, I can tell!" Aunt Gertrude spoke up. "All those crocodiles in the Nile eat boys like you for breakfast!"

"And lunch, Aunt Gertrude," Joe added impishly.

"Don't get smart, young man, or *you* won't get any lunch!" his aunt replied tartly.

Later the telephone rang. Hoping it would be their father, Frank hurried to answer it.

A familiar voice on the other end boomed, "Hey Frank, are you ready for the big one?"

Frank relaxed and grinned. "It's Chet," he informed Joe.

Chet Morton was their best friend. A rotund youth with blue eyes and freckles, he enjoyed eating more than anything. But he had been on many investigations with Frank and Joe, and they knew they could count on him in a pinch. Chet played catcher on the Bayport High baseball team and was inquiring about the upcoming game.

"We're ready for Greenpoint High," Frank assured him.

"Good. I called yesterday, but you guys were out. On another case, right?"

"Right," Frank admitted. "We'll tell you about it when we see you at the game."

Frank and Joe packed their suitcases, then drove to Bayport Field shortly after noon. The team was already on hand with gloves, bats, and baseballs.

Chet was in his catcher's gear, his face mask pushed up on top of his head. He grinned when he saw the Hardys. "Here come the Bayport sleuths!" he called out. "Fellows, let the Hardys pass!"

"It's hard to get past *you*," Joe teased their friend. "You're wide enough to block a Sherman tank!"

"Just enough to cover home plate," Chet replied good-naturedly. "Now tell us about your new case."

The others gathered around. There was dark-haired Tony Prito, Biff Hooper, the star athlete of Bayport High, and Phil Cohen, who liked to read as much as he enjoyed solving mysteries. They listened excitedly as Frank and Joe described the mummy and their adventures in the museum.

"We'll be leaving on the *Admiral Halsey* tomorrow," Frank added. "With the mummy—"

He was interrupted by the sound of a bus pulling into the parking lot. The Greenpoint High players had arrived.

The game began with Frank pitching and Chet catching. Phil played first base, Tony, second base, and Joe, shortstop. Biff was in the outfield.

It was a tense game in which the innings rolled by and neither team could score a run. In the top of the ninth, the Greenpoint slugger came to the plate with the bases filled and two out. The count went to three balls and two strikes. Chet called for a fastball.

Frank kicked his left foot high in the air. His arm came around, and he put everything he had into the pitch. The batter swung and missed!

Joe led off the bottom of the ninth. He slammed the ball in a high arc toward the fence. The Greenpoint center fielder raced back to the fence and leaped into the air with his glove outstretched. The ball cleared it by inches!

Joe circled the bases with the game-winning home run to the applause of the crowd.

"That's Hardy power!" Chet called out. "A shutout for Frank and a homer for Joe! But the game couldn't have been won without a catcher whose name I won't mention. Boy, I must have lost ten pounds! I need food. Otherwise, I'll shrivel like a mummy!"

5

All Aboard!

"We'll pickle you in a barrel of salt water," Joe suggested with a grin. "That way you'll last as long as the pharaohs of Egypt!"

"No thanks," Chet said. "I'd rather have a hamburger."

After a snack at Nick Pappadopolos's diner, the group broke up and the Hardys drove home. The phone rang as they walked into the house. Frank answered.

"How'd you make out in New York?" Mr. Hardy asked.

"It was quite an experience," Frank replied and told his father about the events of the past twenty-four hours. "Is it okay if we go to Egypt in Mr. Salim's place?" he asked.

"I don't see why not." Mr. Hardy chuckled. "I just hope you and the mummy get along and have a nice trip!"

"What about your investigation, Dad?" Frank asked.

"I'm leaving the United Nations tomorrow to fly to the country that's threatened by a radical minority. I've learned that the takeover will be attempted soon. The government of this nation hopes I can crack the conspiracy before then. Sorry, but I still can't tell you where it is. Meanwhile, good luck on your mission!"

Early next morning the boys flew to New York and reported to the Egyptian Museum. The crate holding the mummy case stood on the loading platform ready for shipment to the docks. It was made up of boards nailed into place at each end. Three metal bands running around the crate at the head, in the middle, and at the foot provided added strength.

"The ends of each metal band are sealed together," Colden explained. "Make sure they're not opened until you get to Cairo."

Four men carefully lifted the crate from the loading platform into the back of a van. The Hardys got in with the driver, who eased his vehicle through the museum exit into New York's traffic. A short time later they reached the dock on the Hudson River where the freighter was moored.

An animated scene met their eyes. Longshore-men shifted boxes, bales, and crates along the dock to where cranes and cargo nets could pick them up. Aboard ship, members of the crew guided the crane cables and cargo nets through open hatches down into the hold.

The Hardys went aboard, showed their passports to the first mate, then watched a cargo net lift the mummy crate high into the air and into the hold. Frank and Joe went inside and watched the crate being lowered onto the floor, where members of the crew moved it in position amid a number of con-tainers about the same size and shape.

When it was safely in place, the boys went up-stairs to the bridge and introduced themselves to Captain Baker.

"I'm glad to see you," Baker declared. "I've been informed about you, and you have my permission to visit the hold at any time to see your cargo. I've assigned you to a cabin on the starboard side near the hold to make it easier for you. I hope you enjoy your voyage."

"Are we stopping anywhere along the way?" Joe asked.

"Just once. We'll be headed across the Atlantic to the Strait of Gilbraltar and then into the Mediterra-nean. After passing the island of Rubassa, we get to Cyprus where we'll make our only stop. From there, it's a straight run to Egypt."

"That makes it easy to watch the mummy," Frank said. "It can't go anywhere while we're at sea."

"It would have to be a long-distance swimmer to reach land from the middle of the ocean," the captain said with a grin. "Well, you might as well check out your cabin. It's almost time to put to sea."

Frank and Joe found that their cabin had a porthole and two bunks, one above the other, on the opposite wall.

"I'll toss you for the lower," Frank said, producing a quarter. "Call while it's in the air." He flipped the coin.

Joe called "heads" and won. Happily he sat down on the lower bunk. Frank climbed into the upper and complained about the lack of space.

"You couldn't get a quarter between me and the ceiling," he grumbled. "The mummy has more space than I do!"

"Well, the pharaoh knows better than to sit up," Joe kidded his brother. "Say, the ship's moving. Want to go topside and watch?"

By the time they reached the deck, the *Admiral Halsey* was sailing down the Hudson. The skyscrapers of lower Manhattan fell behind and they passed the Statue of Liberty. Soon the freighter was churning through the waves of the Atlantic. The land disappeared, and they were on the high seas.

"What'll we do now?" Joe asked. "We can't spend all our time in the hold watching the mummy!"

"No need to," his brother agreed. "It's safe. But we should check on it a couple of times a day just to make sure it doesn't get damaged. Let's go down and see that it's secure."

They descended the metal steps into the hold. Before they reached the bottom, Frank suddenly stopped short and grabbed Joe's arm.

"What's—?"

"Sh!" Frank pointed to the left of the hold. Across a pile of boxes and bales stood the mummy crate. A man in sailor's clothing was kneeling beside it! Apparently he had not heard the boys.

"What's he up to?" Joe whispered.

"I don't know, but we'd better find out. Let's try to get down and hide so we can watch him."

Stealthily, the Hardys tiptoed down the steps. But then the freighter lurched in a heavy wave and threw Joe against a pile of boxes. The man scrambled to his feet and turned around. When he saw the Hardys, he darted off between the cargo!

Frank and Joe raced after him. He slipped into a side aisle past a file of automobiles. When the boys reached the corner, the fugitive was nowhere to be seen!

"I'll go left," Frank panted. "You circle around on the other side. Maybe we can trap him between us."

Joe turned right and quickly made his way past the cars. At the end of the line, he moved around to

41

the other side. About halfway down, a mass of crates made him halt.

In the semidarkness of the hold, he heard furtive sounds on the other side. Someone was coming toward him! Joe retreated into the shadows and waited with bated breath. He was ready to jump the man the moment he appeared.

He saw a hand reaching up to the top of a big crate. Quickly he grabbed it and pulled its owner up! Then he gaped in surprise. He was staring at his brother!

"How do you like that!" Joe said in disgust. "We've been stalking each other."

"But we couldn't have missed him," Frank insisted.

Another noise proved he was right. The fugitive suddenly shot from the space between the crates and one of the cars, leaped onto the hood and down the other side, then dashed along the corridor. His shoes rang on the metal steps as he clambered up to the deck.

The Hardys ran after him. They reached topside and saw a sailor swabbing the deck. They ran over to him. He was a burly man whose flattened nose and battered ears proved that he had once been a boxer.

"Who are you?" Frank demanded.

"Butch Londy," the sailor growled.

"What were you doing in the hold just now?"

"I ain't been in the hold. You must be off your rocker!"

"Did you see anyone come out?"

"No! Now buzz off. I got work to do." Londy walked away.

"Stymied again." Frank grimaced. "Either he was in the hold or he knows who was. But we can't tell which. Joe, we'd better get below and see if the mummy's okay."

They found the crate unharmed and decided to go to their cabin. As they walked in, they saw two figures sitting on the lower bunk. Both were all wrapped in bedsheets!

"Welcome aboard!" one of them boomed.

"We've been waiting for you!" the other intoned menacingly and stood up. He was well over six feet tall!

Frank and Joe stared at the two intruders apprehensively and backed toward the door. "Who are you?" Joe demanded. "And what are you doing here?"

"Mummies!" the tall figure hissed. "We're mummies, and we've come to keep you company!" With that, both pulled off their sheets.

Frank and Joe stared in surprise. "Chet and Biff!" Frank exploded. "How on earth did *you* get here?"

Biff grinned. "We got to talking after the baseball game. Since we had no jobs for the summer, we called the *Admiral Halsey* and asked if they needed any extra hands."

"And they hired you a day before sailing time over the telephone?" Joe was incredulous.

"We-e-l-ll," Chet said sheepishly, "we spoke to the captain and told him we were friends of yours. Since we still had our union licenses from the time we worked in the Merchant Marine, he said okay."

The Hardys burst out laughing. "What a great idea!" Frank sputtered.

"I'm the captain's radioman," Biff said, "and Chet's a waiter."

"That suits his style," Joe chortled.

"You bet," Chet said. "See you at the captain's table tonight!" With that, the two left.

At dinner, Captain Baker and his guests were amused at the spectacle of Chet Morton, who wore a waiter's jacket about two sizes too small. He could barely button the jacket across his stomach, and the cuffs fell inches short of his wrists. The shoulders were so tight that he had trouble balancing a tray.

"It was the best we could do for him," the captain said. "Our last waiter was small and thin. So his jacket doesn't fit Mr. Morton too well."

Chet bustled back and forth, serving the courses and carrying empty dishes away. At the end of the meal, he piled the last china and cutlery on the tray, lifted it over his head, and moved toward the galley, trying to maintain his footing as the ship rose and fell in the ocean swell.

He got through the door. Then those at the table heard a terrific crash punctuated by the sound of dishes breaking and silverware hitting the floor.

A moment later Chet peered around the door. He was red-faced and embarrassed. "Sorry about that," he mumbled.

"That's all right, Mr. Morton," said Captain Baker. "It takes every sailor a little while to get his sea legs."

Chet was soothed by the captain's words. He grinned and vanished into the galley.

That night the Hardys went to sleep early. In the small hours, during the freighter's graveyard shift, there was a furious rapping sound at their porthole window. Startled, Frank and Joe sat up.

In the moonlight, they saw a face glaring at them—the face of a mummy!

6

A Raging Storm

Joe leaped out of his bed and Frank swung down from the upper bunk. They rushed to the porthole, but the mummy's face jerked to one side and disappeared.

Frank threw the window open and poked his head through. A slim man in sailor's clothing was swiftly climbing up a rope attached to the railing above! When he reached the top, he vaulted onto the deck.

"We're too late to catch him," Frank said grimly. "He'll be gone by the time we get up there."

"Let's investigate anyway," Joe suggested. "Maybe we'll find a clue that'll tell us who he is. Or perhaps somebody spotted him."

The Hardys dressed quickly and went up on deck. The freighter was plowing steadily forward through the Atlantic waves in the predawn darkness. A light showed on the bridge where the pilot kept the vessel on its course.

Frank and Joe circled around, then climbed to the bridge. "Anything moving on deck?" Joe asked the pilot.

"Not a thing," he responded. "Everyone's asleep, I guess."

The Hardys descended to the deck again and circled from bow to stern and back, past the captain's cabin and the lifeboats. In the darkness, they noticed a man slinking along toward the front of the freighter. They hurried after him and reached the bow just as he did. He whirled around and stared at them. It was Butch Londy!

"Hi," Frank said. "Nice night for a walk."

Londy smirked. "It sure is. This is how I get my exercise."

"What about climbing up and down the side of the ship on a rope?"

"You're a real joker, ain't ya?" Londy scowled.

"How come you're not sleeping?" Frank asked.

"I'm on the graveyard watch. You think I'd go walking for fun in the middle of the night? How come *you're* out here?"

"We're walking for fun."

"Walk all you want, but don't bother me," Londy grumbled, then moved along the deck and vanished into the darkness.

"I can't figure this out," Frank said to his brother. "This is the second time we've been visited by someone wrapped up like a mummy. Maybe the same person. He could have followed us from the museum—I wonder if it's Butch Londy!"

Joe shook his head. "Londy's bigger than the man in the museum. But whoever he is, he's trying to frighten us. I don't think he wants us to go to Egypt. We'd better watch our step or we'll end up overboard!"

In the morning, the Hardys reported to Captain Baker about the mummy face at their porthole.

The captain was shocked. "I have no idea who it could have been!" he admitted.

"Have most of your crew sailed with you before?" Joe inquired.

"Some have, some haven't."

"How about Butch Londy?"

"He's new. Do you suspect him?"

Joe shrugged. "Maybe."

"I'll keep an eye on him," the captain promised.

Later, the Hardys met Biff and Chet. Neither of their chums could tell them anything about the weird episode, but both agreed to keep the sailor under surveillance as much as they could.

"We might even pick up a clue from other people because we're members of the crew," Biff pointed out. "They might say something in front of us that they wouldn't mention in front of you."

Frank nodded. "Thanks for the help, fellows."

The four agreed to meet before lunch and compare notes. Frank and Joe's search had been fruitless, but Biff had hit pay dirt. "Follow me!" he said excitedly. "I want to show you what I found."

He led the way to a lifeboat and raised the tarpaulin. Inside lay a rubber mask shaped and painted like the face of a mummy!

"Our suspect dropped his face!" Frank cried out, picking up the rubber disguise. He turned it over and noticed a tag bearing the word "Luxor" inside.

"Luxor is in Egypt!" he said. "Maybe that's where he got it."

"But we still don't know who he is," Joe pointed out. "Let's set a trap for him. We'll leave the mask in here and keep the lifeboat under surveillance. Then we nab the guy when he comes back for the mask."

"Terrific idea," Frank agreed.

"We'll spell you when we're off duty," Chet offered. "This way we can watch around the clock!"

During the days that followed, the four boys met regularly to see if one of them had learned anything. However, their reports were always negative. The man they were looking for never returned to the lifeboat to retrieve the mummy mask.

"He must suspect something," Frank concluded. "That's why he's steering clear of the place."

The voyage continued without incident. The Hardys checked the mummy crate several times a day and always found it untouched. They also watched Butch Londy. However, the surly sailor seemed to be performing his duties aboard ship like any other member of the crew, and they never saw him do anything suspicious.

Near the Strait of Gibraltar, Captain Baker suddenly ordered all hands to their emergency stations. "We're running into a storm," he announced tersely over the loudspeaker. "Photos from a space satellite show it will be a big one, approaching hurricane force. So batten down the hatches. We'll have to ride it out."

The Hardys volunteered to assist the crew in preparing the freighter for the storm. Chet was released from the galley to help hand out boots, oilskin coats, and floppy hats with brims extending down over the neck to keep the water out. The captain ordered Biff to stand by to radio an SOS if it should be necessary.

Meanwhile, the waves grew higher and higher. The sky became dark, and rain began to fall. Soon the full force of the storm burst over the ship!

The *Admiral Halsey* pitched up and down in the violent, seething swells of the Atlantic. She rolled so heavily from side to side that she seemed about to turn over. Torrents of spray whipped by high winds swept across the deck. The rain fell in sheets, and bolts of lightning flashed through black thunderheads in the sky.

The crewmen clung to the railings as they made their way along the deck. They had to shout at the top of their voices to be heard over the screaming wind, the booming thunder, and the sound of gigantic waves breaking over the bow and making the ship shudder.

Frank and Joe were assigned to help see that the hatch over the hold remained intact. If it went, the Atlantic would pour down into the hold, ruining the cargo and endangering the ship.

Joe was worried about the mummy. "The coffin is bound to be knocked around," he said tensely. "I hope the old pharaoh doesn't break!"

"He's wrapped up pretty tightly," Frank said. "I think he'll—hey, here comes Chet!"

Their rotund pal had been ordered up from his duties belowdecks to help fasten a lifeboat near the bow that was being torn from its moorings by the force of the wind and the waves. He was wearing an outsized oilskin, boots fastened above his knees, and a sou'wester tied by a strap under his plump chin. Water dripped down over his face, and he kept wiping it away by running his hands across his cheeks and his nose.

In spite of the storm the Hardys could not help laughing at Chet's appearance. But instead of joining in with his usual good humor, Chet looked at them mournfully. He felt nauseous and he wished fervently that the violent motion would stop.

"I think Chet's getting a bit green around the gills," Frank said to Joe. Their friend, however, did not give in to his weakness. Bravely he assisted three other crewmen in forcing the lifeboat back into place and they all lashed it to stanchions on the deck.

Chet went to the railing, playing out a rope behind him. It was his job to wind the rope around the railing to give the lifeboat greater stability. He had just finished making a sailor's knot when a tremendous wave broke over the bow and surged along the deck.

The wave knocked Chet off his feet and swept him overboard!

7

Surprise Message

While the Hardys were watching in horror, Chet plunged into the boiling sea! A moment later he came to the surface. His sou'wester had been swept away, and his head bobbed up and down in the waves. Frantically he struggled to keep from drowning, but the oilskin around his body constricted his arms.

Frank wasted no time. He grabbed a life preserver from underneath the railing and tossed it toward their pal. It was attached to a long rope. Frank wound the end of it tightly around his hand.

Joe, meanwhile, had stripped off his rain gear and was about to jump in after Chet. But Frank held him back.

"Don't be foolish! You can't do anything for him down there. Look, he's getting closer to the life ring." Frank clenched his fists tensely as he watched a wave carry the white and red life preserver away from Chet, then brought it closer again.

"Oh, come on, Chet!" he cried. "Grab it!"

For a moment neither Chet nor the life ring could be seen. But then their pal surfaced, clinging to the preserver as tightly as he could.

"Thank goodness!" Frank sighed in relief as he and Joe began to pull the ring toward the ship. Other crew members, meanwhile, had become aware of the accident and pitched in, helping the Hardys to raise their load. Chet clung to the ring with all his might, but his arms were getting weaker and weaker. He was about to let go in utter exhaustion when helpful hands grabbed him and pulled him over the railing. With a gasp, Chet collapsed on the deck.

"Quick, take him inside and dry him off," one of the sailors told Frank and Joe. "We'll watch the hatch for you."

The Hardys half led, half dragged their pal to their cabin. Chet was shivering from the cold water. His skin was deathly white and he felt as if he had swallowed half the Atlantic Ocean.

He tried to speak while Frank and Joe took off his wet clothes and wrapped towels and blankets around him. "Th-thanks, guys. I almost didn't make it!"

"You gave us a pretty good scare, buddy," Joe said. "If we had to lose anyone, I'd rather lose the mummy."

Chet grinned weakly. "Considering what the mummy is worth, I'm flattered!"

By now the storm was beginning to subside. After the Hardys had put Chet into Joe's bunk to rest, they returned to the deck and helped the crew stow away the equipment. The hatches were opened, and soon the *Admiral Halsey* was once again sailing through placid seas.

When they had finished their work, the boys went into the hold for an inspection of the mummy crate. To their dismay, one of the metal bands had snapped open, and a board was hanging loose!

"Frank!" Joe gasped. "Do you think somebody fooled with the crate?"

"Let's see if the mummy's okay," Frank suggested. After inspecting the padding underneath the loose board, he shrugged in frustration. "There's really no way to tell unless we break the other seals, and we're not supposed to do that!"

"Maybe the storm did it," Joe said. "There are other crates that have broken loose, and a couple are slightly damaged over there, see?"

Frank looked just in time to notice a dark shadow

looming in the next aisle behind a huge tractor. The blade of a hatchet appeared over the treads, then a sailor moved around the vehicle.

Butch Londy!

He came toward them, the hatchet half raised in his hands. The sharp edge gleamed wickedly, and he wore his usual scowl.

Frank and Joe automatically stepped apart. If he were to attack one of them, the other would be behind him in a position to launch a counterattack. Tensely they went into a karate stance to avoid the first swing of the hatchet.

But Londy did not swing. "Gotta fix the crate," he snarled. "It's yours, but I'm the ship's carpenter, so I was told to do the repairs for you."

The Hardys were too relieved to say anything. They watched Londy as he pulled a hammer out of his pocket. He nailed the board tight again, then drew the ends of the metal bands together and twisted them so they would stay in place.

"There," he growled. "That'll take care of your mummy."

"How do you suppose the board got loose?" Frank asked. "Could someone have done it deliberately?"

"How should I know?" Londy walked off, whistling a tune and swinging his hatchet.

The voyage went smoothly after that. The

freighter passed through the Strait of Gibraltar into the Mediterranean Sea and continued on past Spain, France, and Italy. Rounding the headland of Greece, it entered the eastern Mediterranean.

Numerous Greek islands appeared over its bow and then dropped astern. Frank and Joe followed them on a map provided by Captain Baker. "The next island coming up is Rubassa," Frank observed.

"Never heard of it," Joe admitted.

"It used to be part of the British Empire," Frank told him. "Now it's independent. The people speak English as far as I know, and quite a few Americans live there."

He had scarcely finished when Biff Hooper arrived with a piece of paper in his hand. "I have a radiogram for you," he announced. "Pretty high-powered stuff!"

Frank took the message and read aloud:

TO FRANK AND JOE HARDY. CAN YOU COME ASHORE RUBASSA? IF SO, HELICOPTER WILL PICK YOU UP. REPLY WITHIN THE HOUR. CRAIG COMPTON, UNITED STATES AMBASSADOR.

The brothers looked at each other in total bewilderment.

"We don't know Ambassador Compton," Joe spoke up. "What does he want with us?"

Frank scratched his head. "Search me!"

"Well, you don't just say no to an American ambassador!" Biff declared.

"I'm afraid we'll have to," Joe said. "We must stay with the mummy all the way to Cairo."

"Chet and I'll take over for you," Biff offered. "Perhaps Captain Baker will give us more time off. Why don't you ask him?"

Frank shrugged. "Why not?"

They found the captain in his cabin and told him about the radiogram they had received. He read it curiously, then put it down on the table. "I think you should go," he said. "It must have been important for the ambassador or he wouldn't have contacted you."

"But how did he know where to get in touch with us?" Frank wondered.

"Perhaps he called Bayport and Mother told him," Joe reasoned.

"In any case," Captain Baker went on, "don't worry about the mummy. Biff and Chet can take your place. As long as the crate's aboard ship, it will be safe. You have my word on that. Go to Rubassa. You can come back by helicopter if this is a quick mission. Otherwise you can fly to meet the ship at Cyprus or Alexandria."

"Thanks, Captain," Frank said. "We'll go."

The Hardys went to their cabin and made preparations to go ashore at Rubassa, while Biff radioed their acceptance to the ambassador.

Frank was thoughtful while he packed an overnight bag. "We're shooting in the dark on this one, Joe. We have no idea what Ambassador Compton wants. It can't be about the mummy because that has nothing to do with Rubassa. And if he just wants to talk to us about something, why didn't he phone the ship?"

"Maybe he's got a case for us," Joe speculated.

Frank chuckled. "That's all we need—another case!"

They got up on deck just in time to see a small speck in the sky, moving in their direction. As it came closer, the sound of the helicopter's engine, muted at first, became increasingly louder until the chopper clattered over the freighter with a deafening noise.

A bosun's chair was lowered at the end of a long cable. Frank strapped himself in and was whisked aloft, then Joe followed. When both had been safely pulled into the cabin, the chopper veered away from the freighter and roared off toward the island.

"What this all about?" Frank asked the grayhaired pilot who was handling the controls.

"Don't know," he replied laconically. "I got orders to pick you up, that's all."

"Where are you taking us?"

"That I can tell you. I'm taking you to a place on the other side of Loma, the capital of Rubassa."

The island came into view, and the chopper crossed the shoreline. The pilot pointed out the window. "There's Loma now," he said.

The chopper dipped to one side and the panorama of the city became visible. A few relatively tall buildings, eight or ten stories high, stood in the center of the town. Modern high-rises flanked the business district. Beyond, stretching into the suburbs, were houses built in the architecture typical of the Greek islands, mainly oblong shapes of whitewashed stone that shone brilliantly in the sunlight.

Crowds milled around in the streets, and shoppers were entering and leaving the stores. The Hardys could see a policeman directing traffic in the main square. It consisted mostly of motorcycles.

"They go for bikes in a big way," Joe commented.

"They go for all kinds of things in a big way lately," the pilot said dryly.

"What do you mean?"

"I mean, be prepared for anything, because anything can happen on Rubassa."

The helicopter began to lose altitude as the pilot cut power on the outskirts of Loma. He brought his craft down in an empty field outside the city.

The trio got out and walked toward a group of men who were waiting beside a limousine.

"I've got the Hardy boys for you," the pilot announced.

"That's great," said the leader of the group, who introduced himself as Major Martin. "Get into the car, boys. The boss is waiting for us."

Frank suddenly felt apprehensive. "I'm not sure I want to get in. I'd like to see your credentials."

The major took a billfold out of his pocket and showed the boys a card identifying him as a member of the U.S. Embassy. The card bore his picture and the seal of the U.S. Government.

"Satisfied?" he demanded.

"Yes," Frank had to admit.

"Then get in."

Three of the men occupied the front seat of the limousine while two sat on the jump seats facing Frank and Joe. The pilot returned to his helicopter and took off just as the driver started the engine of the limousine.

Frank still felt suspicious. Was Major Martin's identification a forgery? Had they walked into a trap?

"Where are you taking us?" he asked.

A smile curled around the major's lips. "You'll find out soon enough!"

8

The Spy at the Embassy

Frank and Joe looked at each other in bewilderment. Each knew what the other was thinking. Were they being kidnapped? Was the radiogram that Biff had received a ruse to get them off the freighter? Did someone plan to do something with the mummy? Was the man in the rubber mask behind the scheme?

The car moved through a small grove of trees and turned off onto a paved road on a cliff along the seacoast. Frank and Joe could see a sheer drop down to enormous rocks in the water. The road wound in and out, and the driver frequently came close to the edge of the cliff at high speed. Joe, who was sitting next to the window, caught his breath.

"I hope this car has wings," he muttered. "We'll be airborne any time now!"

But then the curves in the road ended and it straightened out for several miles along a ledge with a cliff rising on one side and another falling away on the other.

Suddenly the roar of motorcycles could be heard in the distance. Frank nudged Joe and said, "Bikes!" Looking through the window in the back, they could see a dozen cycles closing in on the limousine.

The leader, riding a sturdy Kawasaki, wore a crash helmet with the visor down just like the rest of the gang. He whizzed past the car and cut over in front of it. Several others pulled alongside. Frank noticed that one of the bikes had a twisted left handlebar, evidently the result of an accident.

Suddenly the cyclists veered toward the limousine. The driver pulled to one side to let them pass, but they kept zooming back and forth, pressing the car toward the open side of the road.

"They're trying to force us over the cliff!" Joe shouted.

"Can't you do something?" Frank asked the men in the car.

"No!" Martin barked. "We're not allowed to carry weapons. And if we stop, there's no telling what they'll do!"

The running duel continued at high speed along

the edge of the cliff. The driver of the limousine skillfully steered away from the steep descent to the rocks whenever the cyclists inadvertently allowed him the room, and the men in the car shouted and shook their fists at their attackers.

"They won't get too close," Joe observed, "because they don't want to follow us over the cliff!"

The driver nodded and stuck to the road, which finally led past the cliff into an area of broad fields with grass on both sides.

In front of the car, the leader of the motorcycle gang gestured angrily to his cohorts, then careened down a side road followed by the rest. The sound of their engines died away.

"They gave up!" Joe exclaimed in relief. Then he looked straight at Major Martin. "Friends of yours?"

"Hardly," the major snapped.

Frank felt even more uneasy than before. "What is this, a gang war? And if so, what are *we* doing here? We're not involved in your problems!"

"You're more involved than you realize," Major Martin said with a low chuckle. "Or you will be very shortly."

A tense silence fell again and no one spoke until they had reached the outskirts of Loma. The driver parked in a side street in front of a third-rate hotel. Paint was flaking from its boards, and several windows were broken.

Frank and Joe had no choice but to get out of the car when the men told them to. Reluctantly they followed the strangers into the hotel.

The major flashed his identification at the desk clerk, then they all mounted creaky stairs, went down a dark hall, and paused before a door. Martin knocked.

Footsteps approached, then the door swung open. Frank and Joe gasped in surprise. In the doorway stood Fenton Hardy!

"Hello, boys," he greeted them. "I'm glad to see you!" Then he turned to Major Martin. "Thank you for escorting my sons," he said. "And of course you haven't revealed anything about our mission?"

"Not a word, Mr. Hardy," the major assured him. "But Frank and Joe got an introduction to the conspirators."

Quickly he described how the motorcycle gang had tried to force their car over the cliff.

The detective listened grimly. "They're the conspirators, all right," he declared. "They recognized our unmarked car as an embassy vehicle. No doubt they have a spy in the embassy who alerted them."

Mr. Hardy closed the door as the men departed and ushered Frank and Joe into the room. Two men got up from a battered couch. The detective introduced them as Craig Compton, the American ambassador, and Colonel George Palos, chief of the Rubassa Secret Service.

"I'm glad you could come," Compton stated, shaking hands with the boys. "I thought you might have to stay on that freighter and guard the mummy."

"The mummy's okay," Joe replied. "Captain Baker allowed two pals of ours, who are members of the crew, to watch the crate for us." As they all sat down, he told his father how Chet and Biff had gotten jobs on the freighter.

"Sorry we couldn't let you know what was happening," Compton began, "but spies are everywhere on Rubassa."

Fenton Hardy took up the account. "This is the conspiracy I mentioned over the phone when you were still in Bayport. Rubassa is the country I was working for at the United Nations. I've come here because the conspirators now have the weapons they need. A disloyal member of the Rubassa Mission at the United Nations was involved."

"We have him under arrest," Palos put in. "But he refuses to talk."

"U.S. Intelligence learned that the arms were taken to the nearby island of Milbin," Compton added. "From Milbin, they were transported to Rubassa. When I heard that, I alerted your father."

"And that's when he flew here from New York?" Joe asked.

"Right. The revolutionaries are a small band of conspirators, but they could stage a coup and overthrow the democratic government. We know they plan to ask a foreign power for troops to hold down the people of Rubassa. That would lead to a grave international crisis, and must be prevented at all costs!"

"Where do we come in?" Joe asked curiously. "I'm sure you called us here for a reason."

"You'll be of service to us because you're not known on the island," Palos stated.

"You see," Fenton Hardy explained, "our countermeasures have to be carried out under cover. In order to prevent a panic, the population must not know the danger. That's why we're meeting in this hotel. As you can see, it's not the best in Loma. But we're hoping the conspirators won't suspect us of being here."

"If that motorcycle gang is part of the conspirators, they might have seen us in the car," Frank pointed out.

"I doubt it," Joe said. "They were concentrating on pushing the driver off the road. Besides, it would be hard for anyone to recognize people in the back seat."

"That's true," Fenton Hardy agreed. "What we

had in mind, boys, was for you to go to a place where our other agents can't because they might be known."

"Such as?" Frank inquired.

"A house in Loma," Palos replied. "We suspect it's the communications headquarters of the conspirators. We believe the tenant, who is an Englishman, by the way, receives and sends messages for them."

"How do we get in?" Joe asked. "He isn't going to invite us to go through his house."

"Your father has thought of a plan," Compton replied. "You boys will be plumbers."

"Plumbers?" Frank asked. "You mean we'll have to fix leaky pipes?"

Fenton Hardy smiled. "Not quite, although you'll have all the equipment that plumbers use, including overalls and hats. You'll find everything in a van in the parking lot behind the hotel. You'll look like members of the Plumbers Union when you drive into Loma."

Frank grinned. "As long as it's only a cover it's okay. Because we don't really know how to fix leaks! We'd have to learn first."

"No need for a crash course," Palos assured them and chuckled. "Now, here's what you do. Go to the address on this card. Tell the tenant, Reggie Watson, that Mr. Baldwin has written to you. He's the owner of the house but hasn't lived here for many years. You are to check all the pipes and replace any that look old enough to give him trouble."

"Got it," Joe said.

"When you get in, split up," Palos continued. "That way, if Watson is alone, he won't be able to watch you both. Go though the house inspecting the pipes, and keeping your eyes open for anything that ties him to the gang."

"What do we do after we leave the place?" Frank inquired.

"Call the embassy. We've all agreed that for safety's sake, you won't talk to anyone but me or your father. And be careful. This gang plays for keeps!"

"That's it, then," Compton stood up. "We can break up and—"

"Help!" A sudden scream rang through the hotel. "Help me, help me!"

"Something's happening downstairs!" Frank cried out. "Come on!"

The Hardys raced across the room, wrenched the door open, and shot out into the hall. Then they took the stairs down two at a time.

A man in a leather jacket and crash helmet had the desk clerk by the throat!

9

An Unpredicted Flood

The assailant heard the Hardys bound down the stairs. Glancing over his shoulder, he released his victim and ran out the door before the boys had reached the lobby.

Frank and Joe rushed to the clerk's aid. He was beginning to get his breath back and opened his eyes. Realizing he was all right, the Hardys dashed out of the hotel. The street was empty!

They turned the corner, but still saw nothing. "Leather jacket put on a good disappearing act," Joe complained. "There's no way of telling where he went!"

"I don't know about that, Joe! Listen!"

From the other side of the hotel came the cough

of a motorcycle engine. It was repeated several times.

"He's trying to start his bike!" Frank cried. "Come on!"

The boys ran around the building at top speed and saw the cyclist tramping on his starter. Frank noticed that the left handlebar of his bike was twisted. It was the same machine they had spotted on the cliff road!

Seeing the Hardys, the cyclist kicked his starter desperately. Just then the motor came to life with a roar, and the cyclist varoomed down the street, kicking up a cloud of dust behind him.

Angrily Joe socked his fist into the palm of his other hand. "He got away! Can you identify him, Frank? Colonel Palos might have a mug shot of him."

"No way. That helmet's as good as a mask."

The young detectives returned to the hotel and found Fenton Hardy, the ambassador, and Colonel Palos with the desk clerk, who was on his feet again, rubbing his throat.

"I almost lost my Adam's apple!" he croaked. "I was away from the desk for a moment, and when I came back, that guy was at the safe. When I asked what he was doing, he jumped me. Said he knew Secret Service plans were in the safe and he'd strangle me if I didn't give them to him."

"He made a mistake," Palos commented. "We keep no Secret Service plans in that safe. Still, it means the conspirators know this hotel is our meeting place. We'll have to find another one. I'll send an agent to guard you," he assured the clerk, "until we catch the gang."

"Good idea, Colonel," Compton agreed. "And now we'd better get going. I think Frank and Joe know what to do."

"Yes," Frank admitted. "But what about the fact that one of the conspirators now knows what Joe and I look like?"

"You boys are our best shot at finding this gang before it's too late," responded Compton. "Just be careful, and if you see anyone eyeing you suspiciously, get out fast. He only caught a fleeting glimpse of you anyway, and you'll both look different when you put on your Plumbers Union outfits."

The group left and walked to the hotel parking lot. An unmarked car stood next to a blue van with the wording **LOMA PLUMBING COMPANY** on both sides.

"You'll find everything you need in there," Mr. Hardy said to his sons, "including the key. And here's something else that might come in handy."

He handed each boy a tiny detective kit. "All the officers in Colonel Palos's command carry one of these," he said. "It contains a screwdriver, a tiny knife, a file, and a couple of explosive pellets. If you throw them far enough away from you, they won't harm you but can create a disturbance long enough for you to get out of a tight spot."

Frank grinned. "Thanks, Dad. I hope we don't get into any tight spots."

"So do I. I'm taking your bags to the embassy with me. See you later." He got into the car with the other two men and they drove off while Frank and Joe donned the overalls they found in the back of the van. They equipped themselves with wrenches and screwdrivers and a map, then Joe drove to the address on the card their father had given them.

Before getting out of the van, they agreed that Joe would inspect the basement while Frank would go upstairs.

A genial young man answered the door.

"Mr. Watson?" Frank asked.

"Yes. What can I do for you?"

"The owner of this house has called us and asked us to check the pipes," Frank replied. "Some of them apparently are quite old, and Mr. Baldwin wants them replaced before they give you any trouble."

"Come in," Reggie Watson replied. "I live here with my mother, who is out visiting. I don't mind if you check the basement and the bathrooms, but don't go into any of the other rooms. Mother wouldn't like it."

"Understood," Frank said.

When they entered the house, Joe said he would inspect the basement, while Frank went upstairs. Reggie accompanied Joe, who walked around banging on the pipes with a wrench. "I wish I looked more like a plumbing pro," the boy thought, "but there's nothing I can do except stick to the act."

Circling the basement, he came to a small room that had been erected in one corner of the large cellar. He turned the doorknob. It did not budge!

"No need to go in there," Reggie said hastily. "No pipes in that room. Here, let me show you the washing machine."

Joe felt there was something Reggie did not want him to see in the locked room, but he had no reason to insist on going in. Pretending to examine the washing machine connections, he resumed banging on the pipes at random.

Meanwhile, Frank checked out the rooms upstairs. Suspicious of Reggie's warning that his mother did not want anyone in the bedrooms, he went in anyway.

The first two produced no clues, and there was no evidence that Reggie's mother was living in the house. As Frank was about to leave the second bedroom, he heard a muffled sound in the hall. He stood stock-still. "Somebody's sneaking up on me!" he thought.

Gripping a wrench for self-defense, he hid behind the door and waited. Seconds passed and nothing happened. As the sound continued, Frank peered into the hall. A cat was sharpening its claws on the wall!

He grinned, relaxed, and stealthily entered the master bedroom. There was still no sign of a woman living in the house. But a slip of paper under the bedside lamp caught Frank's eye. Leaning over, he read a telephone number.

Beneath it was a notation: *Hide arms pending further orders from Luxor.*

Frank's heart pounded. The message was clearly a reference to the illegal weapons shipment. But why Luxor? What had the Egyptian city to do with the Rubassa conspiracy?

Unable to figure out the answer, Frank banged the pipes in the bathroom a few times to make them echo in the basement and give Reggie the impression that he was doing his work upstairs. Then he descended to the kitchen and slipped under the sink. He was lying flat on his back when Joe and Reggie came up from the cellar.

"How are the pipes on the second floor?" Reggie inquired.

"Okay," Frank replied. "But I think you may

have trouble with the sink. Joe, take a look at this!"

When Joe got down on his hands and knees and poked his head under the sink, Frank whispered, "I found something. Let's wrestle with this pipe to make it look good, and then get out of here."

"There's something suspicious in the basement, too," Joe whispered back.

Frank clamped his wrench around the bolt at the point where the pipe curved down from the wall and then up into the sink. It seemed stuck, so Frank got a firm grip on the wrench and twisted it. Suddenly the bolt came off!

Whoosh! Water gushed out of the pipe, deluging Frank and throwing spray into Joe's face!

"Put the bolt back on!" Joe cried.

"I can't! I dropped it but I can't move!"

Joe felt around on the soggy floor.

"Hurry up. I'm drowning!" Frank cried out and pressed one hand against the leak and held the other over his face.

At last Joe's fingers closed around the bolt. Frantically he thrust it into position against the force of water gushing out of the pipe. As he screwed it back on, the deluge subsided to a trickle and then stopped.

Wet and bedraggled, the Hardys crawled out from underneath the sink. Water covered the floor around them.

"I wasn't planning to start a flood," Frank said in

embarrassment. "I was just testing the bolt. I didn't expect it to come off so easily!"

"Forget it," Reggie said cheerfully. "I'll mop up."

Frank and Joe went back to the van feeling like fools. "I hope Reggie didn't catch on to the fact that we aren't plumbers," Frank said worriedly.

Joe shrugged. "He didn't seem to. But we sure got wet."

The boys drove to a vacant lot where they took off their overalls and tossed them into the back of the van. They discussed the secret room in the basement of Reggie's house and the message on the slip of paper in the bedroom. Deciding they should report to their father, they phoned the American Embassy, but were told that neither Mr. Hardy nor Colonel Palos was in at the time.

"What do you think we should do?" Joe asked.

"Let's call that phone number I found in the bedroom," Frank suggested.

"Good idea. It must be a number the gang uses. Why don't you imitate Reggie's voice and see what happens?"

Frank nodded and dialed the number. A man answered. "Who is this?"

"Reggie," Frank replied, hoping that his imitation would get by. "I need confirmation of our plans."

"You know we don't discuss that over the phone,"

78

the man said impatiently. "Come to the Beacon."
He hung up.

"Did you hear what he said?" Frank asked. "The
Beacon. I wonder what that is."

"Let's ask a policeman," his brother suggested.

Frank drove to the main square of Loma, where
an officer directing traffic supplied the answer.

"The Beacon is an abandoned lighthouse. Take
this road, turn right when the pavement ends, and
follow the dirt lane straight up. It's near the top of
Beacon Mountain."

Frank, at the wheel of the van, drove as directed.
He took the steep mountain trail, and kept going
until they spotted the lighthouse about a hundred
yards to the right. Since the area below was too
open to afford cover for the van, he drove to a point
higher up the mountain and parked in the woods.

Then the boys sneaked down to the lighthouse,
which was only two stories high since it stood on a
plateau overlooking the Mediterranean. The trees
and bushes surrounding it indicated that it had been
abandoned for years. The sea was no longer visible
from where it stood.

Frank pointed to five motorcycles lined up along
the base of the structure, half-hidden in the bushes.
One of the machines had a twisted left handlebar.

"The guy who tried to strangle the desk clerk
must be inside!" the young detective whispered to

his brother. "The same one who tried to push us over the cliff."

"And he's got some of his friends with him," Joe responded in the same undertone. "We'd better be careful."

The thick underbrush gave the Hardys all the cover they needed to sneak up to the lighthouse. Carefully parting a bush with their fingers, they peered through the open window into the single lower room of the building.

Five men were seated in wooden chairs around a table. All were wearing leather jackets, rough pants, and heavy boots. Their crash helmets lay on the table in front of them.

"Only a few more days," one of the men said admiringly to a tall, dark-haired companion, "and you'll be Michael Linos, dictator of Rubassa!"

The boys recognized his voice. He was the man who had told them over the telephone to come to the Beacon.

Linos grinned. "Liberator, Roger, not dictator. Anyway, I'll sure be glad to quit my job as porter at the American Embassy. It's been one big pain in the neck!"

Joe nudged Frank. "He's the spy Dad was telling us about!"

Frank nodded but did not reply as Linos continued, "And then I'll get myself a new bike. That twisted handlebar makes for a very uncomfortable ride!"

"How come you never replaced it after the accident?" another man inquired.

"Superstition," Linos replied with a chuckle. "When Colonel Palos and his agents almost caught me and I had to ride across that chasm to the other side of the mountain, I vowed to keep the bike that served me so well until the revolution was over. Too bad I took that awful spill and twisted the handlebar."

The Hardys heard the sound of a motorcycle thundering up the road. The driver careened through the bushes, parked the bike at the head of the line along the wall, and entered the lighthouse.

He walked into the room and removed the crash helmet. A mass of blond hair tumbled out, framing the face of a woman in her late twenties!

Frank and Joe gasped. She was Norma Jones, the cook from the Egyptian Museum in New York!

Norma smiled at the men. "You can start your revolution any time now!" she said triumphantly.

10

The Runaway Van

"All the weapons have arrived," Norma Jones informed the gang. "They're already stored in the basement of Reggie's house."

"That's it!" Joe murmured. "The secret room in the basement. I knew there was something fishy when he didn't want me to go in there!"

"I phoned Reggie," Norma went on, "to hold the arms until further notice."

Frank elbowed Joe and whispered, "The message on the piece of paper I saw in the bedroom!"

"Excellent," Linos congratulated Norma. "You've done a great job finding money and buying weapons for us."

"It took some doing," Norma admitted.

"How'd you manage?" one of the men asked.

Linos smiled. "Tell Carlo about it. He just got here yesterday and wasn't in on the details."

"I sold the stolen artifacts from the Egyptian Museum to a private collector," Norma explained. "Then I bought the arms on the international market and had them shipped to Milbin, where the government is friendly to us. From there it was a short run into Rubassa. We did it at night with small boats and slipped past the coast guard every time."

"You'll be paid well for your services," Linos promised. "As soon as I liberate the island."

"That's what we want," Norma declared. "Money. Lots of it."

Frank wondered who the "we" referred to. He looked at Joe, who shook his head to indicate he had no idea either.

She spoke again. "I'll be leaving Rubassa soon. So I won't be riding with you anymore. You can have my bike, Mike."

"Oh, thanks!" Linos responded enthusiastically. "It's the fastest cycle on the island. I'll make good use of it. Of course," he chortled, "I'll have all the motorcycles I want when the revolution is over."

The conversation in the lighthouse turned to personal matters and Frank grabbed Joe's arm, pulling him away into the bushes.

"We'd better get to the embassy and tell them about this gang!" he said excitedly.

Joe nodded. "Colonel Palos and his men will have to move pronto before these guys overthrow the government."

The boys sneaked through the woods back to their van and Frank drove to the dirt road leading down the mountainside. "Those guys didn't hear us coming up," he said, "but I won't take any chances going back. I'll coast down so the motor won't make any noise."

Turning off the ignition, he allowed the van to move under its own momentum on the steep road. The vehicle gained speed and Frank stepped on the brakes to control it.

But nothing happened! Frantically, the boy hit the brake pedal as hard as he could. Again, there was no reaction.

"The brakes don't work!" Frank yelled. "We're out of control!"

The Hardys were trapped helplessly as the van hurtled down the mountainside!

"We have to get off this road!" Frank cried in despair. A cliff loomed on his right, so when an opening of trees appeared on the left, he twisted the wheel violently in that direction. The van crashed through bushes, saplings, and undergrowth. It bounced over rocks and gullies. Finally it came to a jolting halt in a thicket of evergreens.

They scarcely had time to realize they were outside the lighthouse when they heard feet pounding toward them through the undergrowth. Seconds later the five men from the gang surrounded the van. The Hardys were captured!

Another man emerged from the nearby woods. He was Reggie Watson!

A sardonic grin showed on his face when he opened the door to the van. "Well, if it isn't my plumbers! What are you doing out here—playing hooky from the job?"

"We got lost looking for a certain place," Joe replied, his face reddening in anger.

"I know. Our lighthouse," Reggie went on. "Only there isn't a thing wrong with the pipes!"

"What lighthouse?" Joe asked innocently.

"Don't play dumb!" Watson said sharply. "You see, I knew you two were fakes when you caused that flood in my kitchen. So I tailed you here on my motorcycle. While you were listening outside the lighthouse, I disconnected the brakes on your van. Too bad you didn't crash at the bottom of the mountain. This way we'd be rid of you by now!"

"We'll get rid of them later," Linos snapped. "Let's take them inside."

Everyone but Reggie followed him, dragging the Hardys along. When they entered the first-floor room, Norma Jones was waiting. She jumped to her feet when she saw the prisoners, gaping in disbelief.

"The Hardys!" she cried out. "They're detectives. I met them in New York at the museum!"

"What!" Linos thundered, and Norma told the gang about her meeting with Frank and Joe.

"Yes, we had the honor," Frank put in sarcastically, "when the lady tried to poison the two assistant curators with heliomin!"

"It seems they've been on your trail ever since," Linos said tersely. "That's too bad, Norma. It could mean trouble if they told anyone else about their suspicions. And before they can cause any more problems, I vote we finish them off!"

Norma shook her head. "Let's hold them here. They're worth more alive than dead!"

"Why bother?"

"Because their father is Fenton Hardy, the famous American investigator from Bayport. He may be after us, too. If so, we can blackmail him into giving up or else he'll never see his sons again!"

Linos nodded. "You have a point. But I don't want to take both of them right now. Let's lock one in the tower until we need him. If we don't, he can stay there forever!"

Two gang members pushed Joe upstairs into the

small room at the top of the lighthouse. They tied his hands and feet and tossed him into a corner. Then they slammed shut the heavy wooden door behind them, turned the key in the lock, and went downstairs again.

"We'd better get going," Linos commanded. The five men took Frank outside and pushed him into the van, which Reggie Watson had moved out of the undergrowth. He had been busy reconnecting the brakes. While he was finishing up, the gang stood around waiting. Norma, who was the last to leave the lighthouse, joined them.

One of the men leaned on the side of the van, watching their prisoner through the window. Now and then he turned to his companions, adding a word or two to the conversation. During one of those moments, Frank surreptitiously put his hand into his pocket and removed a tiny pellet from the detective kit his father had given him.

"I sure hope this works," he thought as he casually leaned his left arm out the open window on the other side. Then he quickly tossed the pellet toward the motorcycles.

Boom! The explosion went off, startling the gang members, who turned in the direction of the sound. They started toward the bikes to see if they were all right.

In the split second that his captors were occupied

by the explosion, Frank wrenched open the van door, leaped out, pushed Norma out of the way, and ran into the woods.

"Catch him!" Norma Jones screamed. "Don't let him get away!"

Frank could hear the gang pushing through the underbrush after him. Turning along a gully, he crossed a small hill and found himself in a grove of tall trees with bare patches of ground on either side. Some of the gang were coming up behind him, and sounds ahead told him others were closing in from that direction. Apparently they had split up and he was caught in the middle!

The bare ground beyond the trees offered no cover and they were about to recapture him!

Desperately Frank shinnied up the tallest tree and hid among the foliage. He saw the men come together beneath him. They began a heated argument about where their prisoner had gone.

"He must have taken a different direction!" Linos roared. "We'll have to fan out and beat through the woods till we find him!"

The gang split up into pairs, with Norma joining Michael Linos and Reggie Watson. Soon the sound of their footsteps faded away.

"I'll have to try to get Joe," Frank thought frantically and slid down the tree. Quietly he hurried to the lighthouse. No one seemed to be around, so he rushed up to the second floor. The gang had left the key in the lock, and, with a sigh of relief, Frank opened the door.

Joe was elated. "How'd you manage—"

"Sh!" Frank said. "Tell you later." He severed Joe's bonds with his miniature knife, then the two tiptoed down the stairs as fast as they could. There was still no sign of the gang.

"We'll make a beeline for the van," Frank hissed. "Let's hope the keys are still inside and Reggie has finished fixing the brakes!"

They ran toward the blue vehicle. Just as Frank climbed behind the wheel, he heard voices in the distance. The gang was coming back!

Frantically he started the car. The engine came to life and with a roar the young detective drove off, leaving nothing but a cloud of dust behind. Just before turning down the mountainside, he gingerly tested the brakes. They worked!

"Thank goodness!" Joe exclaimed. "If we had to drive off that road again, we might land in the middle of the rebels for a second time. Where are we going?"

"To the embassy," Frank replied. On the way, he gave his brother a terse account of how he had outsmarted the criminals.

"Boy, am I glad we had those emergency kits," Joe said. "I tried to reach mine, but they tied me up so efficiently that it was impossible. You were lucky you could use yours."

Soon they reached their destination and parked the van in the lot. Then they rushed to the gate and identified themselves. They were ushered into the ambassador's office, where Fenton Hardy was briefing Mr. Compton about a meeting he had had with an official of a friendly nation.

"I learned that the spy in the embassy is a Rubassan," he declared. "But I still don't know who he is."

"We do!" Frank remarked. Quickly he and Joe told everything they had discovered.

"Excellent work!" Mr. Hardy said and smiled proudly at his sons. "Now I'll take it from here." He picked up the phone and called the Rubassa Secret Service. After a brief conversation, he declared, "Colonel Palos and his men are on their way to Reggie Watson's house. They'll pick us up in five minutes."

Palos was at the wheel of the lead car. Mr. Hardy sat beside him while Frank and Joe occupied the back seat. Only Ambassador Compton remained behind as the group raced through Loma.

They came to a screeching halt in front of the Englishman's home and rushed up the steps. The front door was unlocked and the house appeared empty. Joe led the way through the kitchen and into the basement.

The door to the secret room was open, swinging on its hinges from the force of a breeze blowing through the cellar window. They peered inside and stared in dismay.

The illegal weapons were gone!

11

Wet Guns

"The gang escaped with the weapons!" Palos said grimly. "We'll have to resume the search."

"Why not go to the Beacon, Colonel?" Joe asked. "Even if we don't find the rebels there, they may have left a clue."

Palos nodded. "You may be right. It's worth a try."

They drove to the lighthouse, but found only some clothes left behind in the gang's hurried departure. Secret Service agents combed through their belongings, but came up with nothing.

"No luck," Palos said in disgust. "We might as well head back for Loma."

The colonel dropped Mr. Hardy and the boys at

the American Embassy, where they reported to Mr. Compton and told him about their futile search.

"We're back where we started," Fenton Hardy admitted.

"Where do we go from here?" the ambassador asked anxiously. "We have to find the gang and the arms before they seize the government!"

An idea struck Frank. "We know the weapons came to Rubassa by way of Milbin Island. Suppose Joe and I go over there tomorrow and see if we can pick up the trail?"

The two men looked at one another, then nodded. "Be careful," Mr. Hardy warned. "You can enter Milbin with your United States passports. However, a dictator runs the island and you'll be kept under surveillance by his secret police."

"Understood," Joe said. "We won't tangle with those guys."

Dusk was falling. The Hardys had dinner and spent the night at the embassy. Early next morning after a quick breakfast, Frank and Joe went to the Rubassa marina. Renting a sleek powerboat, they chugged out into the harbor, passed between two tall rocks standing like sentinels at its mouth, and reached the open sea.

Frank was at the controls while his brother pored over a map spread out on the bow.

"If we turn south," Joe announced, "and go along

the Rubassa coast for five miles, we'll reach a point where it's a short run across the water to Cedura, the capital of Milbin. I suggest we take that route."

Frank nodded. Then he laughed. "You know, I feel a lot better as a pilot than I did as a plumber."

Joe made a face. "You're right. We were closer to drowning in Reggie's kitchen than we are out here!"

They putt-putted along the coast, noticing that huge rocks were a hazard in the shallow water.

"If we hit one of those," Frank said as he skillfully maneuvered around them, "we'll go straight to the bottom."

Suddenly they spotted another powerboat ahead. It moved away from the shore and sailed between the rocks toward the open sea.

"Look out," Joe cautioned. "They're cutting straight across our bow. We're on a collision course!"

"Don't worry," Frank responded. "*They* don't seem to be watching, but I am. We won't hit them. Say, somebody's moved to the stern and is looking at us!"

The figure was holding fast to the flagpole and stared at the Hardys who were coming up rapidly. Both parties recognized each other at the same time.

"Well, if it isn't Norma Jones!" Frank cried out in amazement.

"It's the Hardys!" Norma exclaimed. "Which means a coast guard cutter might be right behind them! We'd better get out of here."

By now Frank and Joe had a clear view of the other boat. They recognized Michael Linos, Reggie Watson, and the rest of the gang. A number of big crates were piled near the stern.

"Those must be the illegal arms!" Joe declared. "They're trying to run them back to Milbin! We've got to head them off!"

While Frank kept on course toward the gang, Joe went to the ship-to-shore radio and sent a message to the Rubassa Coast Guard. He was told a cutter would be on the scene as soon as possible.

"How soon will that be?" the boy inquired urgently.

"I don't know," came the reply. "It's patrolling further south. I'll order it into your area at once."

Meanwhile, the rebels headed straight out from Rubassa in a desperate attempt to outrace the Hardys to Milbin Island. But Frank was too quick for Norma Jones and the gang. Revving up the motor, he made his powerboat skim over the surface of the Mediterranean at top speed. He zoomed in a wide arc that threw spray high in the air and managed to get between the other boat and the open sea.

"Is this such a good idea?" Joe questioned his brother. "There are a lot more of them than of us."

"What else can we do?" Frank asked tensely.

Joe shrugged. He began to rummage in a locker and found a couple of signal flags. Quickly he ran to the stern of their boat and held them high in the air for the expected coast guard cutter to see.

Norma Jones had watched him closely. She called to her associates and her voice drifted back to the Hardys. "We're not going to make it! They're too fast for us and they're signaling the coast guard, just as I thought. Let's turn back before the cutter catches us."

Linos spun the wheel of his powerboat, which made a sharp curve as he reversed direction. Then the gang headed back toward Rubassa. The Hardys followed. Both boats roared along a winding course between the rocks, while Frank swiftly narrowed the distance between them.

Desperately the rebels attacked one of the crates with hammers, ripped the boards off, and withdrew rifles that were quickly handed around. They ran to the stern, lifted the guns, and took aim at the boys!

"Frank, stop the boat!" Joe shouted. "They're shooting at us!"

"Too late!" Frank yelled back. "We'll be on top of them in a minute. Duck!"

They could hear the sound of rifles clicking. Then the members of the gang lowered their weapons.

"I thought these guns were loaded!" one of them bellowed.

"The ammo's in the lowest crate," Reggie shouted. "Get it out."

As he spoke, Linos swerved around a gigantic rock. The next moment he ran directly into a small rock barely protruding above the surface! It smashed a hole in the gang's boat, which started to ship water at an alarming rate. Amid the cries and curses of the rebels, it began to sink!

Frank, meanwhile, had managed to slow down. Cautiously he rounded a bigger rock when his engine conked out.

"Oh, no!" he cried in dismay. He tried starting it again, but had no luck.

"I'll take a look and see if I can fix it," Joe suggested. While he busied himself in the engine compartment, Frank watched the rebels swim ashore and clamber up on the beach. They paused momentarily, gasping for breath, then disappeared into the woods.

"I think I found the trouble," Joe called. "The vibration shook loose a wire. Now try starting the engine again."

Frank did, and the small inboard motor raced to life. "Get a fix on where that boat sank," he called to his brother. "I'll follow the gang to shore."

Joe made a notation for the coast guard so they could retrieve the sunken vessel and its cargo. "What do you plan to do?" he asked his brother. "The rebels are long gone."

"I know. But we're near the foot of Beacon Mountain. They might have gone up to the lighthouse, to change clothes."

"It's worth a try," Joe agreed as Frank maneuvered the powerboat ashore. The boys jumped out and pulled it onto the sand, then they entered the woods and climbed up to the plateau where the lighthouse stood. Stealthily they circled around to where they could move in, using the greenery for cover.

When they arrived at the same place where they had eavesdropped before, they peered through the window. The gang was inside, dripping wet!

Linos paced up and down in agitation. "We lost our guns because of those nosy kids!" he fumed. "And we might even lose our lives, not to mention the rebellion! C'mon! Let's get out of this place. Too many people know where to find us."

"What are we going to do?" one of the men asked.

"We'll have to lie low for a while, then try to get new weapons. The revolution will be postponed, but it'll take place as soon as we recover. I had a new deal in the works already, so things are not as bad as they seem."

"What kind of deal?"

"I can't discuss it now," Linos insisted. "We'd better go upstairs and change our clothes and get out of here!"

Everyone agreed and raced to the top room.

"Frank, we'll have to do something!" Joe exclaimed in an undertone.

"I'll go up after them and lock them in!" Frank hissed. "Just keep your fingers crossed that the key's still in the lock. You wait here in case something goes wrong, okay?"

"Okay."

As quietly as possible, Frank ran into the lighthouse and tiptoed up the stairs. The key was still there! With an inaudible sigh of relief, the boy slammed the door shut and turned the key in the lock!

A confused babble of voices broke out in the room. A chair went over backward as the duped gang members rushed to the entrance. Someone tried to open the door and shouted, "It's locked!" while heavy fists pounded on the wood.

Frank ran outside and rejoined Joe. "Let's run down the mountain and flag the coast guard cutter that's coming our way," he suggested.

As the boys hurried past the lighthouse, they saw Linos glaring down at them through the barred window. The gang members were standing around him.

"The Hardys!" the rebel leader rasped. "They followed us here!"

Frank and Joe paid no attention to him. Instead, they rushed to the shore as fast as their feet would carry them. A coast guard cutter lay in the deep water beyond the rocks, and a launch was drawn up on the sand beside their rented boat.

"Boy, are we glad to see you!" Frank panted when he spotted the skipper.

"We received your message," the man replied. "When we saw your boat, we came ashore to look for you."

Frank and Joe quickly explained what had happened, and the skipper ordered an armed company of his men to land. He led them up Beacon Mountain, guided by Frank and Joe. As they reached the lighthouse, they could see the gang trying to force the bars on the window.

"That won't do you any good!" the skipper shouted. "Come out with your hands up!"

A file of sailors entered the building and mounted the stairs. One of them unlocked the door and the rebels had no choice but to come out one by one.

Linos was furious. "Hardys, I'll get even with you someday!" he snarled.

"Don't hold your breath!" Joe advised him.

Reggie Watson was the last person to emerge

from the room. "That's it, sir," a sailor reported to the skipper.

The Hardys were startled. "Are you sure?" Frank queried.

"Quite sure," the sailor replied. "Why?"

"Because Norma Jones isn't here! She must have escaped!"

12

Tunnel of Horrors

"There's no point in hunting for her in these woods," the skipper decided. "She could be anywhere by now."

The boys had to agree. They accompanied the officers and their prisoners back to shore, then took their boat to Loma while the coast guard cutter chugged off with the rebels.

When Frank and Joe reached the marina, they turned in the rented craft and rode in a taxi to the American Embassy, where they found the ambassador, Colonel Palos, and their father discussing the latest events.

"You already know?" Frank asked in surprise.

"The coast guard phoned us," Mr. Hardy said

with a smile. "You boys have done excellent work. The capture of Linos and his gang means that Rubassa is now safe from dictatorship."

The ambassador nodded in agreement. "American Intelligence has known for a long time that if the Rubassa rebellion failed, the supporters of democracy on Milbin Island would be encouraged to remove their dictator from power. We hope this will happen soon."

"Meanwhile, my case is finished," Mr. Hardy added. "Frank and Joe, you'd better rejoin your freighter. The *Admiral Halsey* reaches Cyprus tomorrow noon. Ambassador Compton will make arrangements for you to fly to Nicosia before it docks."

"But Dad, we haven't found Norma Jones yet," Frank objected.

"We will be looking for her," Colonel Palos assured him. "I have taken too much of your time already and wouldn't think of keeping you here now that the rebels are caught."

The following morning, he escorted the Hardy boys to the Rubassa airport, where they boarded a turbojet to Cyprus. They reached the Nicosia dock just as the freighter was being tied up.

"I wonder if our mummy missed us," Joe said with a grin as they climbed the gangplank.

Frank chuckled. "Let's ask Chet and Biff!"

Their friends met them at the end of the steps.

"Welcome back!" Chet cried. "The pharaoh hasn't stirred while you were gone. We took good care of him."

"Thanks, Chet," Frank said. "We appreciate that."

"How'd you make out on Rubassa?" Biff inquired. "Did the ambassador want you to find a crook for him?"

"No, he wanted us to prevent a revolution," Joe replied.

Chet's eyes popped out. "A what? Don't tell me you guys finished off a whole rebel army!"

"No," Frank assured him. "There were only six of them. But with a good supply of weapons, they could have taken over that small island."

"And guess where they got the money to buy the guns," Joe put in. "From the sale of the pharaoh statuettes they stole from the Egyptian Museum in New York!"

Quickly the brothers filled their friends in on the latest events. Chet and Biff were impressed and proud of the young detectives and congratulated them over and over.

"Now I'd like to see our friend the pharaoh," Joe said finally.

"Come with us," Chet offered. "We'll lead you to him."

The four descended into the hold and found the

mummy crate untouched. Then they reported to Captain Baker, who was on the bridge supervising the unloading of the cargo destined for Cyprus.

When they had finished their story, he smiled. "You did a wonderful job. You deserve a day off!"

"Oh, we wouldn't leave the *Admiral Halsey* while it's docked," Frank said. "Someone could carry the mummy right off the ship!"

The captain shook his head. "Not if you wait until all the unloading is done. Around three o'clock many of the crew will have shore leave, and I can station a man who's on duty right next to the crate. Chet and Biff will remain aboard, too, and can double-check on your ancient friend."

Frank and Joe did not need further convincing. In the afternoon they strolled around Nicosia in the hot sunshine, enjoying their leisure. Most of the people they saw spoke Greek and wore Greek dress, but the Turkish minority could be identified by their own language and costume.

"It seems so peaceful now," Frank commented.

"Just as well," said Joe, who, like his brother, recalled there had been much violence between Greeks and Turks on Cyprus. "I'd rather not run into terrorists who throw bombs around like baseballs."

Sampling some of the local snacks, the boys walked through town until they came to an open area where a carnival was going on. The ticket seller called out to them in Greek, held up two tickets, and gestured with his thumb toward the entrance.

"He wants us to go in," Frank interpreted. "What do you say, Joe? Let's see how it stacks up against the Bayport Carnival."

"Okay. I'd like a few zany rides after the heavy stuff we ran into on Rubassa. It'll be a treat to relax."

Joe paid for two tickets, then led the way into the carnival grounds. They heard barkers appealing to the crowds to come in and see the sideshows. A roller coaster roared up and down steep rails and a Ferris wheel lifted its patrons high above the throngs on the ground.

"It's just like our carnival at home!" Frank exclaimed. He bought a guidebook in English and turned the pages while Joe pointed to a gaudy sign portraying a monster with scowling face and clutching hands. Beneath the figure were some words in Greek and Turkish punctuated with enormous exclamation marks.

"I'd hate to meet him in a dark alley," Joe commented, gesturing toward the monster. "Does the book say anything about this sideshow? What do those words mean?"

Frank flipped the pages until he saw an illustration of the sign. "Here it is. The words mean *Tunnel of Horrors*. It's a boat ride through a dark tunnel and you get to see vampires, zombies, and were-wolves. Want to go?"

"Why not?"

Frank bought the tickets, and the boys entered a flat-bottomed boat with two seats large enough to hold six people. They sat side by side in the back. The man in charge gave the boat a push onto a flowing current kept on the move by an electrical generator.

The boat floated about five yards, then was carried by the current into the black mouth of the tunnel. Almost at once, a vampire screamed at them from an illuminated niche on one side of the tunnel. Its fangs were bared and its eyes blazed.

Joe felt the hair stand up on the back of his neck. "That's too real for comfort," he muttered. "It's enough to give anybody the jitters."

"Whoever makes these things is pretty good," Frank agreed. "They're only rubber, cloth, and plastic with lights around them. And they're held in place by wires. But you'd think they were alive and ready to jump at you."

Further on, a zombie materialized in the darkness, glowering at them. By now Frank and Joe were enjoying the thrills of the Tunnel of Horrors.

"Hi," Joe called to the zombie. "What's your name—Frankenstein?"

"He's shy," Frank said. "Doesn't want to tell us."

The boat drifted into darkness again. The flicker of a light told them they were about to confront another monster. This time it was a snarling werewolf.

"There's Rover," Frank laughed. "I bet he's somebody's family pet."

"He's lost, Frank. Let's take him home. Aunt Gertrude can use him for a watchdog. She wouldn't have to worry about burglars with him in the house."

The boat floated on through the darkness, and the Hardys saw more of the horrors advertised in the tunnel, next being a spider the size of a Saint Bernard perched in the middle of a web. The mechanism controlling it caused the insect to rush to the edge of its web, where it seemed to be drooling venom from its snapping jaws.

"It's the last one, I think," Frank said.

"No, there's one more," Joe declared. "See that light on the ledge up ahead? I wonder what kind of monster this one is."

"Oh, I don't believe it!" Frank cried out. "Look who's here!"

A weird face became visible, a face with cloth bandages wound around. A couple of black eyes glared through holes in the wrapping.

Frank and Joe doubled over with laughter. "Hi,

Tut!" Joe addressed the apparition as the boat drifted up beside it. "Come aboard! There's always room for a pharaoh!"

Suddenly the mummy's face lurched forward and the light illuminating it snapped out. In the darkness, the strange figure leaped into their boat. A moment later they felt the sting of tear gas spraying into their faces!

Frank and Joe collapsed into the bottom of the boat, gasping, wheezing, and shielding their eyes from the chemical. The intruder thrust a piece of paper into the pocket of Frank's shirt, then jumped onto the ledge on the opposite side and disappeared into the darkness.

The boat drifted out of the Tunnel of Horrors into daylight at the point where the ride ended. There was no sign of the mummy anywhere.

It took the Hardys some minutes to recover from the blinding effects of the tear gas. Finally Joe gasped, "He was the guy who looked through our porthole! He must have followed us from the ship."

He leaned over and picked up two objects from the bottom of the boat. One was a flashlight and the other a pencil-sized tube with a button near one end.

"He used the flashlight to illuminate himself on the ledge," the boy declared. "And this tube is a miniature tear gas gun. That's what he sprayed us with. He must have dropped them when he jumped out of the boat."

Frank reached into his breast pocket and pulled out a piece of paper. "I felt him put something in there," he said, holding up the note. "Joe, listen to this! It says, 'Remember the mummy's curse. Get away while you can!' "

The Hardys looked at one another, wondering what it could mean.

"That guy's warning us," Joe said. "He followed us from the freighter and sneaked into the Tunnel of Horrors while we were getting the tickets."

"And he's still in there now!" Frank exclaimed. "Come on, we'll trap him."

Making sure no one was watching, he stepped out of the boat onto the ledge used by the maintenance men who kept the tunnel in working order. Joe followed, and they edged their way back into the darkness. Moisture from the water moving along below them made their footing slippery.

"I wonder how deep it is," Frank muttered over his shoulder.

"Not deep enough to drown in," Joe said. "But you could sprain your ankle if you slipped."

They inched along the ledge. A boat filled with laughing teenagers floated past, then silence fell again. Moving along the wall, Frank came to a door.

Pausing for a moment to be sure of his footing, he turned the knob and pushed the door open.

Light shone in their faces and they found themselves going out of the tunnel into the daylight of the carnival grounds. There was no sign of the man in the mummy mask!

13

The Empty Coffin

"Foiled again!" Joe exclaimed angrily. "No doubt our friend walked right out of this door and disappeared in the crowd five minutes ago!"

Frank nodded. "Maybe he's been here before and knew the setup."

They got back to the *Admiral Halsey* a half-hour before it was scheduled to leave. The crew had already returned and were getting the ship ready for departure.

"Let's see if we can find Biff or Chet," Frank suggested, and the boys started to look for their friends. They found both of them in the galley.

"Guess what happened!" Chet called out when he saw the Hardys.

"Oh, oh," Joe said apprehensively. "Is something wrong with the mummy?"

"Not the mummy. But the mask is gone!"

"Disappeared!" Biff confirmed. "That weirdo must have sneaked back to the lifeboat when we were busy watching the crate in the hold."

"That doesn't surprise me," Joe declared. "He took it and followed us into Nicosia. We saw him at the carnival!"

"But he gave us the slip," Frank added.

Chet and Biff were astounded when the Hardys told about their ride through the Tunnel of Horrors.

"I wonder if he came back to the ship," Chet said. "If he didn't, and one of the crew is missing, we'll have an idea who he is."

"Good thinking," Frank said. "Suppose you two check out the sailors while Joe and I have a look at the mummy."

Once more the Hardys found the crate untouched. Later they met Chet and Biff again, who reported the crew all present and accounted for.

"I'm sure the culprit is a seaman," Frank declared. "But which one?"

The *Admiral Halsey* continued on course in its voyage across the Mediterranean to Egypt. The four youths from Bayport kept the lifeboat under surveillance, hoping the man they were after would return to hide the mask again. But he never did.

Finally Egypt came into sight. The freighter entered the seaport of Alexandria in the Nile delta and tied up at dock. The gangplank was lowered, Egyptian officials went aboard to talk with Captain Baker, and the sailors of the ship opened the hatch over the hold. Egyptian stevedores, or longshoremen, moved cranes and cargo nets into position and lifted boxes, bales, crates, automobiles, and other items out of storage onto the dock.

Frank and Joe were waiting outside for the mummy crate to appear while Chet and Biff were in the hold to signal the Hardys when the case had been picked up by the crane.

"Here it is!" Joe called out as an oblong container appeared high in the air and swung over the dock area. The crate hung there, swaying from side to side at the end of a cable while the operator of the crane prepared to lower his burden to the ground.

Suddenly the cable began to fray! Some of its strands broke under the weight, and the cargo lurched to one side!

"It's going to fall!" Joe shouted to the crane operator in alarm. "It'll be smashed if it hits the ground!"

The man sat frozen for a moment, as if afraid that another movement of his machine might make the cable snap. Frank ran to an untended cargo net.

Starting the motor, he quickly raised the net up and eased it under the crate.

Just then the cable snapped in two. The crate tumbled into the net, and Frank lowered it to the dock.

Joe ran over to him. "Take a bow!" he said fervently. "You just saved the pharaoh!"

Frank wiped perspiration from his brow with his fingertips. "Well, I was lucky that this cargo net was on hand."

The stevedores lifted the crate from the net and carried it to a small truck with the words **CAIRO EGYPTIAN MUSEUM** on both sides. Frank and Joe introduced themselves to the driver, who invited them in halting English to ride with him.

Just then Chet and Biff ran down the gangplank. "Hey, you can't leave without saying good-bye!" Chet complained.

Frank laughed. "Of course not, especially since you helped us so much during the trip. We really appreciate it, fellows."

"Too bad you aren't going back with us," Biff spoke up. "This time it would be fun only!"

"We're flying home as soon as we've delivered the mummy," Joe said. "And we'll beat you to Bayport!"

Frank and Joe climbed into the truck while their

friends waved, then returned to the ship. The driver started the engine to begin the long run from Alexandria on the Mediterranean coast up to Cairo at the apex of the Nile delta.

He maneuvered his truck through the outskirts of the Egyptian capital and finally entered Independence Square. The Hardys saw a broad, open area made up of concentric circles where ten avenues came together. Buildings occupied by departments of the Egyptian government stood on one side of the square with the Nile–Hilton Hotel nearby. There the boys dropped off their bags, then continued to the Cairo Museum, which was located at one corner.

The truck stopped and the driver motioned for the boys to get out. A staff member was waiting and greeted Frank and Joe with a friendly smile.

"My name is Mahmoud Salim," he said. "I am in charge of our new acquisitions. I understand that you know my brother, Najeeb Salim, who works for the Egyptian Museum in New York."

The Hardys admitted knowing Najeeb without voicing the fact that he was a suspect in the statuette theft.

"We came in his place because he was ill," Joe said.

Mahmoud Salim nodded. "He telephoned me

116

about the heliomin in his coffee. I am happy to say he is getting better."

Two men came out of the museum and carried the mummy crate inside. The boys and Salim followed.

"This is where the crate will be opened," the Egyptian said when they had reached a large room in the basement. "Professor Fuad Kemal will be in charge. He is our expert on mummies. However, he is not here at the moment. The case is safe here, so I suggest that you—how do you say—kill time by viewing the museum. I would call to your attention the beautiful objects from the tomb of the Pharaoh Tutankhamen."

Frank and Joe went upstairs and walked through halls lined with artifacts of ancient Egypt. They saw stone panels covered with hieroglyphics, statues of pharaohs and queens of Egypt, and pictures of war, hunting, and domestic life.

Suddenly a blaze of gold met their eyes. They had come to the Cairo Museum's most famous exhibit, the treasures of Tutankhamen.

First, they noticed a great sarcophagus that resembled the one they had seen in New York except that it was much more splendid. The image of the pharaoh was sculpted onto the lid of the case, the eyes half-closed in a passive stare.

117

Instead of a scepter, one hand held a shepherd's crook, symbolizing the fact that the pharaoh was the shepherd of his people.

"King Tut looks like he's going to sleep," Joe commented.

Frank chuckled. "Maybe he's had a hard day at the palace."

Joe pointed to the forehead of the ornate headdress, where a Nile cobra was portrayed in an upright position as if prepared to strike. "This looks just like the one we saw in the New York museum."

The Hardys admired the golden masks of Tutankhamen, golden images of gods, golden furniture, and golden carvings representing life in ancient Egypt.

Then they paused before the mummy of Tutankhamen. The head was distorted by a backward extension of the skull. The nose was flattened, the teeth protruded through the lips, and the skin was crinkled like wax paper.

Joe shuddered at the sight. "Embalming didn't do *him* much good!"

A voice behind them spoke up. "I think the embalmers made a mistake!"

Turning, they recognized Mahmoud Salim. "I believe they used too many fluids," he continued. "Instead of preserving the corpse, they caused it to deteriorate." He paused for a moment, then smiled. "I have come to inform you that Professor Kemal has arrived and is waiting in the basement. If you will join him, our new mummy can be removed from its sarcophagus."

The three returned to the downstairs room where the Hardys met the professor. He was a stout, short fellow wearing the fez of modern Egypt, a high red hat with a flat top from which a black tassel dangled. He had a pleasant smile, and greeted the two Americans cordially.

"I expected to see Najeeb Salim," he declared. "But I am pleased that the mummy had two escorts instead of one. It made the journey from New York so much safer."

Kemal ordered his workmen to begin. Using chisels, they broke the metal seals around the crate. Then they hammered the top boards loose, placed them to one side, and removed the padding that protected the sarcophagus. At last they reached the mummy case itself which was wrapped in burlap held in place by three leather straps.

The men lifted the sarcophagus out of the crate onto the floor. They undid the straps and pulled the burlap away. The image of a pharaoh gazed at them from the lid of the case.

"They sure didn't take any chances when they

wrapped the coffin in New York," Frank commented. "I had no idea it was packed in so many layers!"

Kemal rubbed his hands together with glee. "This is a wonderful moment for all Egyptologists. I long to look upon the mummy of the pharaoh who once ruled here on the banks of the Nile. Open the case!"

The workmen loosened the lid and took it off. Kemal gasped, and the Hardys stared in disbelief.

The sarcophagus was empty!

14

The Trapdoor

"Where is the mummy?" Kemal exploded.

Frank scratched his head. "I have no idea, Professor. We made sure the crate was guarded while it was on the ship, and the seals were not broken."

"You mean the crate was never tampered with?" Kemal demanded angrily.

"One of the metal bands snapped during a storm," Frank replied. "We figured the violent motion of the ship caused it."

"Could somebody have opened the crate and removed the mummy during the storm?" Kemal asked.

"I don't think so," Joe replied. "It was tough to keep on your feet with the freighter pitching up and down. How could anyone have opened the case, removed the mummy, and then put identical seals on?"

An idea struck Frank. "Perhaps someone substituted this crate for the real one in Alexandria!"

"But how is that possible!" cried Joe. "We never let it out of our sight!"

"I know." Frank turned to Kemal. "Let me call the ship. The radioman is a friend of ours. I'll have him ask Captain Baker to order a search of the freighter."

Kemal gave his consent and Frank phoned the *Admiral Halsey.* Quickly he told Biff about their problem, then hung up.

"The ship will be checked right away," he announced. "Biff's going to call back and let us know if they found anything."

The group waited anxiously until the phone rang. "Nothing here, Frank," Biff reported. "There's no mummy crate aboard. However, something's happened that might interest you."

"What's that?"

"Butch Londy jumped ship! He's gone!"

Frank gritted his teeth. "I wonder if he has our mummy."

Crestfallen, the Hardy boy reported the news. He told the professor about the difficulties they had encountered and the missing seaman who had acted so suspiciously during their journey.

"The real crate must have been smuggled ashore," Kemal declared. "You will have to hurry to Alexandria to find it!"

"We will go right away, sir," Frank said. "But I suggest you call the police."

"I will," Kemal said. "And I expect to hear from you soon!"

The boys walked out into Independence Square and sat down on a bench.

"I never felt like such a fool!" Frank complained. "How could a thing like this have happened?"

Joe shrugged unhappily. "I don't know. We watched that crate as closely as we could."

"I don't think going to Alexandria is such a good idea," Frank said. "Whoever has the mummy has probably taken it out of town already."

"Frank, let's go to Luxor!" Joe exclaimed suddenly. "The mummy mask we found in the lifeboat had a Luxor tag in it. And the paper you saw in Reggie Watson's house in Loma mentioned Luxor. Since there is a connection between the Rubassa case and the museum thefts, maybe we'll find a clue in Luxor!"

Frank jumped up. "Great idea! How do we get there?"

"Let's try the hydrofoil. I saw an advertisement for it when we drove by a travel bureau just down the street."

The boys were informed that the hydrofoil to Luxor would be leaving in three hours. They decided to use the extra time for a visit to the Cairo bazaar.

Soon they found themselves in the most romantic quarter of the Egyptian capital. Shops lined both sides of the main street. Colorful banners waved in front of places selling everything from luxurious cloth to strange medicines. Vendors wandered along the street carrying large baskets of bread on their heads. Men pushed heavy carts loaded with baskets, hats, and shoes, while women carried jars of oil. There was a mingling of traditional Egyptian costume with modern Western dress.

Merchants called their wares from the doors of their shops as the Hardys went along.

"Look at this!" Frank exclaimed as he stopped at one shop and pointed to a row of masks hanging from a pole outside. They were replicas of mummy faces!

As the Hardys stared in fascination at the display, the proprietor came out to speak to them. He wore a fez and had his hands folded over his stomach.

"I see you are interested in mummy masks," he

said in a soft voice. "There is another inside that you might care to see."

Overcome by curiosity, the boys followed him through the front part of his shop into the back room. A single mummy mask hung on the rear wall.

"Frank," Joe muttered, "that looks like the one the guy on the ship used!"

"It sure does. But it can't be, can it?"

"Perhaps you would like a closer look," the merchant suggested. He bowed and extended an arm toward the mask.

The Hardys moved forward. Suddenly the floor gave way under them and they plunged through a trapdoor!

Landing with a thump, they were stunned for a moment. Then they realized they were in a small, subterranean room lit by a single weak bulb in the ceiling. The door had been pushed shut above them. Solid walls enclosed them except for one place where they could see the outline of a narrow door.

"I doubt it's open," Joe grumbled. "Boy, did we ever walk into this one!"

"I don't get it," Frank said. "We don't know this guy from Adam. What's he want from us? He had no idea we would even come here today."

Joe had approached the door and was just about

to try the knob, when it opened and four men burst inside. One of them was Butch Londy!

Frank and Joe stared at them in surprise.

"You didn't expect me, did you?" Londy grinned maliciously.

"What do you want?" Frank demanded.

"I want to get even!" Londy said softly. "You gave me a hard time on the ship, and I'm giving you a hard time now!"

Realizing they were about to be attacked, the Hardys decided to go into action first. Joe caught Londy in a flying tackle and bowled over the ship's carpenter. Frank seized the Egyptian merchant in a bear hug and wrestled him to the floor. A battle royal raged and the boys used their karate training to overcome their antagonists. Frank pinned the merchant down while Joe got a hammerlock on Londy.

But the other Egyptians grabbed the Hardys from behind. Four against two proved too much, and finally Frank and Joe were overpowered.

Londy rubbed his arm where Joe had twisted it. "You'll pay for this, double in spades!" he snarled.

"Indeed, the price shall be a high one!" the merchant declared venomously as he retrieved his fez from a corner where it had rolled during the fight.

Suddenly another figure came through the doorway—a man wearing a mummy mask. He gave a high-pitched cackle similar to the one they had heard during the night they guarded the mummy case in the New York museum.

Then the man whipped the mask off. He was Ahmed Ali!

"Hardys, I fooled you," he scoffed at Frank and Joe.

"You stole the statuettes from the museum!" Joe blurted out.

"And you tried to frighten us away from the mummy by wearing that weirdo mask!" Frank added.

Ali smirked. "You are correct. I stowed away on the *Admiral Halsey*. I was the one you chased through the hold. But you failed to capture me."

Londy laughed. "I helped him. I told you guys I hadn't seen anyone on deck. But I knew Ali was hiding in the lifeboat. Same thing when he looked through your porthole. The Hardys ain't so smart after all!"

Frank saw the point. "You followed us from the freighter to the carnival in Nicosia, Ali."

The man nodded. "Butch was watching your friends, Morton and Hooper. He got the mask out of the lifeboat when they were not looking. I sneaked off the ship during the turmoil of unloading the cargo at Nicosia. I waited to see if you two would leave. When you did, I followed you all the way into the Tunnel of Horrors."

"Well, at that point we fooled you!" Frank said. "We didn't scare."

Ali scowled. "It doesn't matter. I flew from Cyprus to Cairo to see that nothing further went wrong. I followed you from the museum, and when you came to the bazaar, I arranged with my friend to trap you in his shop."

A light dawned on Frank. "*You* also tampered with the mummy crate when you were hiding in the hold. That's why the metal band was open and the board loose!"

"I did."

"Where's the mummy?"

"Where I wish it to be."

"Which is?"

"We've talked enough!" Londy interrupted. "Let's get this show on the road. I'm in this for money and I want my payoff as soon as possible."

"What about us?" Frank asked.

"You come with us!" Ali put in. "We'll hold you captive in case your father appears on the scene and attempts to interfere with us. Oh yes, we've heard what happend to the rebels on Rubassa. That'll not happen to us. Fenton Hardy won't dare to make a move against us when he learns that his sons are our prisoners."

"And when it's all over?" Joe queried.

Londy scowled. "You'll take a swim in the Nile. All the way down!"

Ali waved to the others and went off by himself. The rest of the gang hustled Frank and Joe out of the shop to the rear where two cars were parked. Two more men, both Egyptians, were already inside one car.

The drivers guided the cars through Cairo to a landing strip on the outskirts of town, where their captors pushed Frank and Joe into a small plane. After everyone was seated, the pilot turned to Londy. "Where to this time?"

"To Luxor!"

15

"It's a Crocodile!"

Frank and Joe stared in surprise, but said nothing. They were sitting in the rear by themselves and watched the plane take off, flying upstream along the Nile. They saw the river cutting through the desert creating a ribbon of green where the land was irrigated. Beyond the cultivated fields, sand and stone stretched to the horizon on either side.

The engine was noisy, and Frank felt safe enough to talk to his brother. "This is a hairy situation," he whispered. "These guys are a bunch of thieves, and we have no idea where they're taking us and for what purpose!"

Joe nodded. "Now I'm sure Ali tried to steal that dagger in the museum when the alarm went off. But

131

how could he possibly have removed the mummy on the ship?"

"Beats me!"

"Hardys, stop whispering back there!" Londy commanded.

With a shrug, Frank and Joe fell silent. The plane flew up the Nile and landed in a desolate part of the desert. Everybody got out except the pilot, who said he had to get back to Cairo.

Minutes later a small battered bus trundled up the road. Its fenders were dented, the tires were worn smooth, and the engine backfired even worse than Chet Morton's jalopy.

"That model must date from the year one," Frank said.

"King Tut rode in it," Joe grumbled.

"That'll do for you guys!" Londy snarled. "Get in. And sit in the middle where we can keep an eye on you. Don't try any funny business or we'll toss you into the river!"

The Hardys climbed into their seats. Two members of the gang were behind them, while the rest sat up ahead, guarding the front door of the bus.

The driver started the vehicle and drove back along the desert road, the surface of which was stone overlaid with sand. Frank and Joe watched a landscape of small hills, valleys, and gulches glide by. Night was falling, and the panorama outside became an eerie pattern of objects and their shadows.

Frank had noticed earlier that he was sitting next to the emergency exit. According to the posted instructions, it could be opened by thrusting a metal bar to one side and pushing the window outward. Frank had an idea. Surreptitiously he elbowed Joe and gestured toward the exit. Then he looked down at his hands. His brother caught on at once. Both held their hands in their laps and began to communicate by sign language.

When Frank finished telling Joe his plan, he leaped to his feet, levered the bar aside, and kicked the emergency exit open. At the same time, Joe pulled out the pencil-shaped tear gas gun that he had found in the boat going through the Tunnel of Horrors.

The men in front and behind the boys had jumped up and were rushing toward them, only to be hit by sprays from Joe's tear gas gun. They retreated, gasping and choking for air. Coughing violently, they turned away from the boys, clutched their throats, and rubbed their tearing eyes.

The bus driver was startled by the commotion behind him. He slowed the vehicle and looked over his shoulder to see what it was all about. At that moment, Frank and Joe leaped through the emergency exit. Luckily they cleared the road and fell into the soft sand beside it. They somersaulted forward head over heels to break the force of the momentum, then managed to get up on their feet unhurt.

"Come on!" Frank hissed. "We've got to get away from here pronto!"

While they hurried off in the darkness, the bus driver managed to come to a stop about a hundred yards further down the road. Angrily he shifted into reverse gear and careened back at top speed. As he hit the brakes, the gang piled out of the bus, shouting frantically.

"Where did they go?" Londy yelled.

"It's too dark to see!" the Egyptian shopkeeper replied.

"Well, spread out and search for them!" Londy bellowed. "They can't be far. Maybe we'll get lucky and find one of them broke a leg when they jumped."

The Hardys had run up a shallow valley between two hills and heard the gang calling out behind them.

"We've got to shake them!" Joe panted.

"That means we'll have to get out of this valley," Frank responded. "It's the obvious route for anyone to take."

The Hardys cut to the side over one of the hills. When they crossed the crest, they were silhouetted against a rising moon.

"There they are!" Londy cried. "After them!"

Frank and Joe dashed down the hill and circled the base in the direction of the bus. They came to a gulch where a stream had once cut a narrow tunnel through a sandstone cliff. Quickly they ducked into the tunnel and lay prone, panting from their run and hoping they would not be discovered.

They heard the gang coming down the hill. "I hope they don't guess we doubled back toward the bus," Frank thought.

As if in reply, Londy shouted, "They wouldn't run to the bus! Go the other way!"

Frank sighed with relief. "Let's check the bus," he said to Joe. "Maybe the driver left the key inside."

When they reached the vehicle, however, their hopes were shattered. The key was not in the ignition. Apparently the driver had taken it along.

"Let's run back to our hiding place," Joe urged. "We'll have to get out of here before those creeps come back."

In a flash, the Hardys jumped down the steps and ran to the tunnel with only seconds to spare before the gang trooped back.

"How do I explain that the Hardys got away?" Londy complained. "Ali isn't gonna like it!"

He was still grumbling as he and the others passed just above the tunnel where the boys lay hidden. A little while later Frank and Joe heard the bus start, then the sound of its motor died away as the gang drove down the road.

The young detectives crawled out of their hiding place. "Lucky they didn't have a bloodhound," Joe commented, "or they'd have found us for sure."

Frank nodded. "Question is, where do we go from here?"

Since they had no idea where they were, they decided to follow the desert road.

"We can hitchhike if a car comes along," Joe observed.

"Crank up your thumb," said Frank, who had noticed lights in the distance. "There's one!"

They stood by the side of the road, each holding out his arm. A Western-make car materialized out of the darkness. Its headlights picked up the Hardys standing in the classic hitchhiking stance. The driver stared at them, but whipped past without slowing down.

Joe dropped his arm. "How do you like that?" he complained. "You'd think the guy could have given us a ride."

Frank chuckled. "Well, I guess it's legmobile for us."

They spent the night walking and resting in between. There was no sign of life around them, and they were cold and hungry. As soon as the sun rose, however, it became unbearably hot and their mouths felt parched and dry.

Frank fought back a wave of panic. Would they ever make it to the next town? It could be another twenty or thirty miles away!

Joe was dragging his feet and finally came to a halt. "I—I don't think I can go much further," he said hoarsely.

"Let's rest awhile," Frank agreed. "Right after we go around that next bend, okay?"

Joe nodded wearily. When they rounded the corner, a glimmer of water became visible.

"The Nile!" Frank cried out in relief.

Despite their exhausted state, they broke into a run and tumbled down the riverbank. Eagerly they threw themselves on their stomachs and drank the cooling water in large gulps.

After that, they lay back, recuperating and staring up into the cloudless blue of the Egyptian sky.

Finally Joe stood up. "I crave food," he stated. "And over there are a bunch of houses. Must be a little village downstream. Maybe we can get something to eat and rest for a few hours."

"I sure hope so," Frank declared emphatically.

When they reached the village, they found nobody who could speak English. But they managed

137

to make their meaning clear in sign language and obtained a meal and the use of two cots in a private house that served as the village inn.

Sometime later they awoke, more or less refreshed. Trying to find out where they were, Joe spoke the word *Luxor* to the innkeeper, who pointed down the Nile and raised three fingers.

"He must mean three kilometers," Frank interpreted. "Less than three miles."

They started to walk alongside the river. At one point they looked back and noticed a sail billowing in the wind on the Nile. Others appeared strung out behind it. A number of wide-bodied boats with triangular canvas sails on slim, towering masts came into view. Each boat was steered by a single man and was loaded with barrels of grain and oil drums.

The Hardys stopped to watch the procession.

"They sure know how to sail against the current," Joe said admiringly. "And the wind. It's the sail that does it."

"And practice, too," Frank added. "The Egyptians have had a lot of practice. They've been doing this for centuries."

The boys saw the boats disappear, then continued their hike in the direction of Luxor.

Suddenly the soft loam of the riverbank crumbled under Joe's foot. He lost his balance and tumbled into the water!

"This is a great time for a swim," Frank kidded him.

Joe tried to scramble up the bank, but the slippery mud made him fall back. He thrashed around, trying to hold his footing.

Suddenly, a long, dark form appeared behind him. It moved toward the boy, rippling the surface as it came closer.

Frank turned pale. "Joe!" he cried. "It's a crocodile! It's coming after you!"

16

The Deserted Temple

Frantically Joe struggled for a toehold that would enable him to climb up the bank to safety. Too late! The long black form closed in on him. Horrified, Frank expected the crocodile to open its jaws and crunch Joe between them!

Joe felt a bump. He looked down into the water and broke out laughing. "Your croc is a floating log!" he announced. Using it to steady himself, he eased out of the river and onto the bank. He sat down, emptied water out of his shoes, and squeezed as much as he could from his clothing.

"Sorry for the scare I gave you," Frank apologized. "I know crocs don't usually come this far down anymore. But I thought this one might have rambled past the High Dam at Aswan by mistake!"

"That's okay," Joe replied. "But I think we ought to walk along the road from now on."

The boys scrambled up the riverbank and soon came to a sign in Arabic with the word *Luxor* in Western lettering underneath. They continued to the edge of a modern town built at the site of ancient ruins.

Frank hesitated. "The gang might be around here looking for us. Let's disguise ourselves."

"There's a place that sells native clothing," Joe said, pointing to a fez in a small store window.

"That's what I had in mind."

Joe grinned and pulled out his wallet. "Maybe I can get rid of some of my soggy money here!"

The boys went into the shop and emerged ten minutes later wearing voluminous gowns over their Western clothes and headdresses with bands of cloth falling to their shoulders. By drawing the cloth together with one hand, they could cover their faces.

Joe took a few long strides. "It's tough to move in this getup," he declared. "How do the Egyptians do it?"

"I guess it takes practice," Frank replied. "Don't give up."

After walking for a few hundred yards, they settled into an easy gait indistinguishable from that of the Egyptians they passed. They followed the crowds in one particular direction—to the ruins of an ancient building marked by four statues, two standing and two sitting.

A bus disgorged about twenty tourists led by a native guide. Frank and Joe were just about to walk past them, when they noticed Ahmed Ali among the visitors!

Instantly, they pulled their headdresses across their faces.

"Let's stay with this group and see where they go," Frank whispered.

The tourists gathered around the guide, who began to describe the surroundings. "These statues are of the Pharaoh Ramses the Second, who lived more than three thousand years ago. Follow me and we will see more."

The boys tagged along through Luxor as the guide pointed out the rest of the ruins. At the end, he told the tourists to return to their bus. "We will now go to see the Temple of Karnak. It is a mile from here along the Road of the Rams. Or rather, what remains of the Road of the Rams."

"Let's go to the temple, too," Joe whispered to Frank. "Think we can get away with boarding the bus?"

"The guide would spot us," Frank replied. "Every tourist guide knows how many people are supposed to be in his group. But it's only a mile. We can walk and catch up with them later."

Frank and Joe were able to find their way to the ruins of the Temple of Karnak. Its rows of massive columns towered high in the air.

The guide was in the middle of his talk when the boys arrived. They paid no attention to his lecture. Instead, they looked for Ahmed Ali and watched him closely until the guide announced that the group now had a half-hour to wander through the area on their own.

The tourists dispersed, and Frank and Joe shadowed Ali, who walked slowly around the temple. Behind a column with part of a wall attached, a man was waiting for him. *Butch Londy!*

Carefully, the Hardys sneaked around the pillar to a point where they could listen to the men's conversation.

When Ali heard that the boys had escaped, he was furious. "You should have watched them better!" he hissed. "They are extremely dangerous to us!"

Londy sounded defensive. "Like I say, they had this tear gas gun. How was I supposed to know that? Anyway, me and the others, we ain't seen 'em around here. I guess they got lost in the desert."

"Let's hope so," Ali barked, "because we want to go ahead with our plan. This is what we'll do—"

Ali stopped as Frank, leaning forward to hear better, stubbed his toe against the base of the column.

"What was that?" the Egyptian demanded, listening intently for a repetition of the noise.

The Hardys froze, Frank holding his foot where it was and flattening his palm against the column to keep from falling on his face.

At last Londy broke the silence. "It wasn't nothin'. Lots of stones around here. One must've fallen from that crossbeam up there. I'd just as soon get out. And I will, once we divvy up the proceeds."

Ali nodded. "To get back to what I was saying, this is what we'll do. Our meeting is scheduled for tonight. We'll get together in this temple at twelve o'clock sharp, when I'll have the final orders."

"Okay," Londy said. "I'll be here." He went off and Ali returned to the tourists who were milling around the bus. A short while later the vehicle departed with the group.

"Joe, we'll also go to the midnight meeting," Frank declared.

"Of course! But first I have to get out of these clothes. They're still damp."

"Let's find a place to stay in Luxor," Frank said.

They took a public bus to a hotel and paid for a room. Frank flopped onto the bed and closed his eyes. Joe followed suit and both boys slept until early evening. Then Joe went to the laundry room where he washed and dried his ordinary clothing.

Frank, meanwhile, had also changed into his regular pants and shirt and turned on the television. A newscaster was describing the state of tourism in Egypt and the film showed an air view of the monuments of Luxor where the boys had just been.

Just then there was a knock on the door. "Joe must have forgotten his key," Frank thought and got up to let his brother in. But when he opened the door, the face of a mummy glared at him!

Frank stood transfixed for a moment, staring at the black shiny eyes set deep in the bandages that wound around the head. Then he noticed the Egyptian clothes the mummy was wearing and the truth dawned on him. With a quick grasp, he pulled the mask off its face. Joe grinned at him.

"I really needed you to scare me like that!" Frank exploded, but then had to laugh at the prank. "Where'd you get the mask?"

"I met a boy from Oklahoma in the laundry room," Joe said. "It's his." He motioned to someone who stood next to the wall, out of sight. "Come on, Lee, meet my brother Frank. Frank, this is Lee Mason."

A pleasant-looking blond youth a few years older than the Hardys stepped into view. He smiled apologetically. "When Joe saw my mask, he couldn't resist," he explained.

"Come on in," Frank said. "Or even better, how about we all go and have some dinner?"

"Good idea," Joe chimed in. "Just let me change my clothes."

A short time later the three boys sat in a small, native restaurant and talked amiably during their meal. Lee told them about his travels in Egypt. "I'm an archeology student," he explained. "I saved all the money I made working as a waiter at night so I could come here. It's a great place if you're interested in old ruins."

"I know," Joe said. "Ruins and mummies!"

When they had finished dinner, Lee said, "I've rented a sailboat for a moonlight ride up the Nile. Why don't you come along? It would be fun."

Frank shook his head regretfully. "Sorry, but we have an appointment tonight."

The trio parted, and the Hardys went back to their room. Donning their Egyptian clothes, they left the hotel by the freight elevator at half-past eleven. They covered the mile to the area around the Temple of Karnak at a rapid pace, then moved slowly amid the ruins and looked around cautiously to avoid being caught off guard.

They sneaked through the darkness into the temple. Total silence reigned over the mighty monument as moonlight slanted along the rows of columns, making them appear even taller than they were.

"This place gives me the creeps," Joe whispered.

"Sh!" Frank said and pointed to a crevice in the stone. "Let's hide in there. We'll have a good view of the corner from that spot."

Soon, stealthy figures converged from different directions. When everyone was present, Ahmed Ali motined for silence.

"We won't complete the deal here," he began, causing the gang members to mutter angrily.

"Why not?" Butch Londy demanded. "We got a right to the money!"

"Of course," Ali responded diplomatically. "But our client didn't want to bring the money to Luxor. We will have to accompany him to Cairo, where he'll pay us after safe delivery of the goods. It'll take a little extra time, that's all."

"What do we do now?" Londy demanded.

"We're going to meet our client in the Valley of the Kings, right now!"

"The graveyard across the river?"

"The tombs of the pharaohs," Ali corrected Londy. "Let's go."

"Too bad we don't have the Hardys," Londy snarled.

Ali chuckled. "We have something better. The mummy!"

17

Valley of the Kings

The gang nodded in agreement. Then Ali spoke up again. "Is the boat ready? If so, I'll meet you there and bring the mummy."

"It's ready," Londy said. "We'll be waiting to ferry your pickup across the river."

The meeting broke up. Londy and the others walked toward the Nile, while Ali went in another direction.

Joe nudged Frank. "We'd better follow him."

Frank nodded. "But we'll have to keep far enough back or he'll spot us."

Ali was only a dim outline in the darkness when the Hardys took up their pursuit. He never realized he was being shadowed. Quickly he strode out of the temple and continued on into the desert. Finally he came to a pickup truck, which was parked in a gully, and climbed into the driver's seat.

Frank and Joe ran forward and reached the vehicle just as Ali started the engine. Nimbly they pulled themselves up into the back and hid under the tarpaulin that covered the rear. Underneath they found an oblong case about five feet in length. The mummy's coffin!

Ali picked up speed. Circling around Luxor and the ruins, he drove to a secluded spot on the Nile. A scow, a long flat-bottomed boat, lay in the water tied to stakes driven into the riverbank. Two cars were already aboard the vessel.

Londy and his men were waiting when Ali pulled up. The Hardys, peering out from under the tarpaulin, took in the scene as the Egyptian came to a halt near the scow.

"Clear the way so I can drive aboard!" he called out, then carefully guided the truck onto the boat. Members of the gang untied the ropes, and with long poles pushed the scow away from the riverbank. Londy started the motor and headed toward the opposite side of the Nile.

To the Hardys, who were still hiding under the tarpaulin in the back of the pickup, the voyage seemed endless. At last, two gang members leaped ashore with the ropes and tied the scow in place.

The cars drove off, then the truck. Londy, who was in one of the cars, waited for Ali to pass him, then tailed the pickup.

"They don't trust Ali," Frank whispered. "They're keeping him in between so he can't get away."

"Good idea, too," Joe muttered. "I don't trust him either."

Lifting up the edges of the tarpaulin on both sides of the mummy case, they strained their eyes to see in the moonlight.

The caravan was driving through a barren landscape. A narrow, dusty road led between the cliffs and steep hills. The rubble of archeological digs lay everywhere—mounds of sand and rock, and boulders of enormous size. The pickup jounced up and down, swaying from side to side as the wheels careened over rocks or slipped off piles of loose sand.

"This is a pretty jolting ride," Frank whispered. "Let's look in the crate to see how the mummy is bearing up." Together they managed to tilt the lid up.

Two black artificial eyes stared at them through the bandages of the ancient pharaoh's wrapped body. But there was only a slight resemblance between this mummy and the one Frank and Joe had seen at the museum in New York!

Both boys realized instantly that this was not the mummy they had been asked to escort to Egypt!

Replacing the lid gingerly, they stared at each other in total disbelief.

When the group came to a stop, clouds momentarily covered the moon, enabling Frank and Joe to slip out of the pickup. Hitting the ground face downward, they slithered away in a panther crawl and stopped behind a small hill near enough to let them see and hear what was happening.

They heard Ali get out of the truck, and as their eyes became more accustomed to the dark, saw a car arrive with Londy at the wheel. Moments later all the men crowded around Ali.

"A partner of mine is hiding in one of the excavated tombs," he announced. "I must give the signal."

He took a flashlight out of the glove compartment of the pickup, then pointed it toward a cliff, at the foot of which lay mountains of rubble from the dig. Ali snapped the light on and off three times in quick succession, then twice, then three times again.

The same signal was returned from the mouth of the excavation, then a figure emerged and walked toward the group.

Joe gasped. "It's Norma Jones!" he whispered to his brother. "So this is where she came after escaping from us on Rubassa!"

"She's here to get money for a fresh supply of weapons," Frank whispered back.

When Norma was told that the Hardys had gotten away, she was furious. "They ruined my plans on Rubassa! They can do it again!" she hissed.

"Don't worry," Ali said. "They're lost somewhere in the desert. Besides, we'll be through with this deal in no time flat."

"I hope so," Norma grumbled. "Well, let's see the pharaoh. He's worth a lot of money to us."

Londy and another man lifted the tarpaulin from the pickup and tossed it aside. Then they eased the mummy case out and placed it on the ground. All the gang members gathered around as Ali and Londy removed the lid.

Norma Jones gloated. "That's just what we need," she said. "It's in wonderful condition. A little while longer and we'll make the deal!"

Ali smiled. "Let's put the lid back on," he said to Butch Londy.

"Okay," the sailor replied. "But where's our client? What's taking him so long?"

"He's driving up from Cairo," Norma replied. "He wants this for his private collection, and he doesn't care where it came from or how we got it. I've sold him other art objects before. It's perfectly safe because he keeps them hidden in his house."

"I wonder whether he bought the stolen pharaoh

figures from the New York museum," Joe whispered to his brother.

"Probably," Frank replied.

At this moment a pair of headlights became visible in the desert behind the boys. Norma Jones blinked the signal with her flashlight, and the car turned in her direction. The boys were right in the middle of its path!

"We'll be killed!" Frank hissed. "Let's run over to the tombs!"

They were about to rise to their feet and take off when the driver swerved to avoid a large boulder at the end of the hillock behind which they were hiding. His headlights shifted to the left.

Joe grabbed Frank's arm. "There's no point in running now. The driver didn't notice us."

"Right. We're safe where we are. Let's see who he is."

The car made a half circle and came to a halt beside the gang in a cloud of dust. The driver, a man wearing a fez, got out and turned around.

Frank and Joe stared. He was Professor Fuad Kemal of the Cairo Museum!

18

Stranded on the Nile

While the Hardys gaped in utter disbelief, Kemal greeted the gang. He asked to see the mummy, and after inspecting it, he rubbed his hands in delight.

"It is in excellent condition," he said. "It will be a choice addition to my private collection. I intend to have two mummies standing beside the window where they will show to their best advantage."

"Two mummies?" Butch Londy asked. "You must really go for these critters."

Kemal nodded. "Norma made it possible for me to buy another one, the one Frank and Joe Hardy were supposed to deliver to our museum. Which reminds me, you do have the Hardys, don't you?"

"They're lost in the desert," Ali said cautiously.

"Fine," Kemal grunted. "Now we will drive to my house in Cairo where I will pay for the mummy. You understand, this is necessary for my protection. After all, the truck could get hijacked on the way! Many things of that sort have happened lately. Unfortunately, there are too many crooks in this world!"

Frank and Joe had to suppress an ironic laugh at Kemal's last remark. Joe ducked his head low behind the hillock to stay out of sight and took a deep breath that filled his nose with dusty particles of sand.

The irritation made him want to sneeze. He twitched his nose in an effort to remain silent and squinted his eyes. When this failed, he pushed his knuckles hard against his nostrils. This, too, was in vain.

Before he had a chance to warn Frank, he sneezed loudly!

The gang whirled around, glancing in the direction of the noise. "Somebody's out there!" Norma Jones hissed. "Grab him!"

Londy moved forward followed by his men.

Thinking quickly, Frank got to his feet. Under his breath he said urgently, "Let's pretend we're natives out for a walk!" The boys drew the flaps of their headdresses together and strolled boldly within view of the gang.

Londy stopped as they came near. He peered at them malevolently through the darkness of the desert broken only by eerie moonlight.

Norma Jones snapped on her flashlight. In its beam, she inspected the two figures in native dress.

"It's all right," she whispered to Londy. "They're Egyptians, probably on their way home. I don't think they noticed what we're doing."

Stifling another laugh, Frank and Joe moved casually within a few feet of her, bowed slightly, and continued on, deliberately walking slowly to avoid suspicion.

"We should stop 'em!" Londy was worried.

"That would only make them suspicious," Norma replied. "Then they might go to the police when they get to Luxor."

"We could do 'em in!" the sailor growled. "Bury 'em in one of these tombs. That's what tombs are for, ain't they?"

"And what happens when they don't return home?" Norma retorted sharply. "Their families will go to the police. Either way, we'll have the cops after us. Is that what you want?"

"I guess not," Londy replied in an embarrassed tone.

That was the last Frank and Joe heard. Feeling secure, they took to their heels and ran off in the darkness. They kept to the narrow road along which they had ridden in the pickup and made their way back toward the Nile.

Frank finally slowed to a walk. "It's at least a couple of miles," he said. "Let's not get puffed out too soon. Besides, it looks as if we'll have to swim across the river, so save your breath."

Joe had an inspiration. "We can take their scow, Frank. They left it tied to the bank. It must still be there."

"That's a terrific idea! We'll make the gang pay for our passage to the Temple of Karnak."

They hurried along through the desert, walking and running to pace themselves, and finally reached the spot where they had come ashore in the pickup. Two members of the gang were lying on the ground asleep near the stakes that held the scow in place at the riverbank.

"They must have been left here to guard the boat," Frank said. "But they're not doing a good job. I just heard a snore."

"Let's sneak the scow away from them," Joe suggested. "You take the stake on the right, and I'll take the one on the left. All we have to do is lift up the loop of each rope and we're off."

"Okay. But first I'm getting rid of this Egyptian outfit. It's too confining."

"Me, too. We don't need it anymore."

The boys removed their headdresses and gowns

and tossed them aside. Then they eased their way down the riverbank to where the stakes were. Slowly and gingerly they lifted the ropes.

Frank's heart skipped a beat as the guard near him moved uneasily in his sleep and appeared on the point of waking. However, the man settled back into a deep slumber. Holding his breath, Frank worked the loop up along the stake, freed the rope, and laid it in the scow. He stepped aboard and picked up the pole used to push off from the bank into deep water.

Joe also got his rope clear and put it inside. As he was about to follow it, he glanced at the guard nearer him. The man was watching him with wide-open eyes!

Instantly, Joe turned and leaped onto the scow. The man scrambled to his feet with a cry of alarm that wakened his companion. The pair rushed forward and, as Frank poled away from the bank, jumped into the river and waded toward the boat.

Raising the pole, Frank struck the first guard in the chest, knocking him off his feet and leaving him to thresh around in the water. The second man waded closer, but he was left behind clutching at empty air as Joe quickly started the motor. The scow chugged out into the Nile.

"Wow! That was a close call!" Joe said.

"And we're not home free yet," Frank replied,

listening to the irregular drone of the boat's engine. "It's missing a lot!"

They were well out in the river heading for Luxor when the motor suddenly died. The boys tried to start it again, but to no avail.

The swift Nile current took control of the scow, which drifted downstream until it hit a sandbar with a thump.

"We're stuck!" Joe cried morosely. "Now we'll have to swim the Nile after all."

"Unless we can hitch a ride!" Frank pointed into the distance, where a white speck on the surface of the river was growing larger and larger as it approached in the dawn.

"That's a sailboat," Frank observed. "Let's see if we can flag it down."

He took off his jacket and raised it high on the pole. The skipper of the approaching vessel adjusted his sail in the high wind and veered in the direction of the sandbar.

Joe was the first to recognize him. "Lee Mason! He must be coming back from his nighttime sail!"

The young man from Oklahoma stared in surprise when he saw his new friends. "Well, I'll be!" he cried out. "What in the world are *you* doing here?"

"We're sitting on a sandbar." Joe chuckled. "Do you think you could give us a ride?"

"Of course. Hop aboard."

The Hardys transferred to the sailboat, then Lee pointed to the scow. "What do you want to do with this?"

"We can leave it here," Joe said. "The harbor patrol will pick it up."

"That's what you get for turning down my invitation," Lee said. "If you'd gone with me instead of striking out on your own, you wouldn't have gotten stranded."

"It's not that simple," Frank said. "We were chasing a bunch of crooks. Matter of fact, the scow is theirs."

"Crooks?" Lee's eyes popped. "Are you detectives?"

"Just amateurs," Frank said modestly. "Now if you could get us to Luxor pronto, we'd appreciate it."

"I'll be glad to. My ship really travels fast in this wind."

The three boys took turns at the tiller since the Hardys were experienced sailors. Lee was on duty when they reached the dock, and he eased the boat into a slip. Then he went to get his deposit back from the marina, while Frank and Joe raced to their hotel. Frank called the Cairo police and asked to speak to the chief. After identifying himself, he was connected with the officer's home.

The chief had been alerted earlier by Fuad Kemal

161

about the missing mummy and was astonished to hear that the curator himself was involved in the theft.

"He and the gang are on their way to Kemal's house where he intends to pay them off," Frank concluded.

"It is hard for me to believe that a prominent citizen of our town is a criminal!" the chief said. "But do not worry, we will check out your story."

"It's true!" Frank urged. "If you want a reference confirming that my brother and I are amateur detectives, you can call Chief Collig of the Bayport Police in the United States!"

"I shall do this," the chief agreed. "And then we will have a welcoming party ready for the professor and his gang of thieves!"

19

The Welcoming Committee

"The police are staking out Kemal's house," Frank told Joe as he hung up the phone. "They're hoping he'll walk right into their trap."

"I'd like to be in on it!" Joe said. "Maybe the mummy we were supposed to bring to Egypt is at his house!"

Frank nodded. "From the way Norma talked, I couldn't tell if he had bought it already or was going to buy it."

"Trouble is, how can we possibly make it to Cairo in time? Even if we rented a car, we couldn't catch up with the crooks."

Just then there was a knock on the door. Joe opened it to let Lee Mason in.

"Did you find your criminals?" he asked excitedly. "After you told me that story I couldn't sleep, tired as I am."

"We called the police and they're staking out the crooks' destination," Frank said. "But we won't be able to get there in time. It's in Cairo, and the gang has a head start on us."

"Hey, I know a guy in Luxor who owns a plane!" Lee volunteered. "He flies tourists around Egypt. Maybe he'll take you to Cairo."

"That's a terrific idea!" Frank exclaimed. "What's his name?"

"Abdel Jimad. He has an American-made four-seater. Got his pilot's license in the States. I've been up with him. If you want to, I'll call him for you."

"Please do!"

Lee phoned the pilot and apologized for waking him up. Then he explained the situation and Jimad offered to take the Hardys to Cairo as soon as they could make it to the small airstrip where he kept his plane.

Gratefully, the boys said good-bye to Lee, promising to get in touch with him once they were all back in the United States. Then they went to the airfield and met Abdel Jimad, who was already there. He was a young man wearing corduroy pants, a green blazer, and dark glasses. Frank edged into the seat next to him, while Joe sat in the back. A few moments later, the plane took off.

Circling over Luxor, Jimad straightened his aircraft into a flight down the Nile toward Cairo. In the rising sun, they could see how the river created a ribbon of green through the desert. Irrigation systems carried its water to fields on both sides. In many villages, the houses were built in the desert away from the river.

When Joe asked why, Jimad said, "The reason is to keep all the irrigated land for agriculture. The population can live in the desert, but fruit and grain cannot. So, the people move into the sand, and their crops get the water."

They flew above the highway between Luxor and Cairo that paralleled the Nile. Traffic was sparse.

"There aren't many cars," Frank noted.

"Not like in the United States." Jimad chuckled. "We don't have as many cars or use as much gasoline!"

At one point where the river made a slight bend to the right and then to the left, the Hardys saw a complex of ruins extending for several miles. "That must have been some city," Joe guessed.

"It is Amarna, built by the Pharaoh Ikhnaton," Jimad replied. "Your city of Washington was built as a new capital. Ikhnaton built Amarna for the same reason, only about three thousand years earlier."

Amarna fell behind, and the flight continued down the Nile. Joe noticed a pickup truck moving along the highway at top speed. One car was ahead of it, two others brought up the rear.

"That looks like the gang we're after!" he exclaimed. "Jimad, can you drop a little lower so we can see them better?"

The pilot nodded and went into a shallow dive.

"It's the gang, all right," Frank burst out. "I recognize the tarpaulin over the mummy case in the back of the pickup!"

"The lead car is Kemal's," Joe added, "and the two behind are the ones we saw Londy and his crooks driving."

By now the plane had roared past the four vehicles and started to loop upward again. "Anything else you'd like me to do?" the pilot asked.

"No, there's nothing we can do now that we've identified the gang. We can't tail the pickup in a plane. Just drop us off at Cairo airport, please."

The delta of the Nile came in sight, and soon Abdel Jimad landed. The Hardys paid him, congratulated him on his skillful flight, and took a taxi to police headquarters.

"Our highway patrol has been radioing reports on the gang," the chief revealed. "We are not having them picked up because Professor Kemal might

166

pretend he is bringing the mummy to the museum. We wish to catch him red-handed at his house."

"We'd like to join the stakeout," Frank declared.

The officer nodded. "You boys have done such good detective work, you have the right to be there. You may come with me."

A number of unmarked squad cars drove to Kemal's house in a suburb of Cairo. Plainclothesmen kept watch at strategic points nearby.

At last the professor arrived and drove into the driveway and around to the back, closely followed by the pickup and the other two cars. As soon as the gang had gone inside, the police converged on the house and rang the doorbell. When Kemal answered, the chief thrust a search warrant into his hand and arrested him. The other officers burst through the door and cornered the rest of the gang in the living room. Frank and Joe followed.

"The Hardy boys!" Norma Jones screamed. "I thought they were lost in the desert!"

"I should've done 'em in!" Londy snarled at Ali. "But you wouldn't let me. This is the last job I ever do with you!"

"Londy," Frank said, "this is the last job you do with anybody. Egypt has laws against stealing mummies. You'll spend a lot of time in jail. All of you will."

The Hardys, helping the police search the house,

came upon Kemal's private collection in a large room at the rear. In one corner, they recognized the five pharaoh statuettes stolen from the New York museum. Panels representing scenes of hunting and war hung on the walls, and stones marked by hieroglyphics lay on shelves. But there was no trace of the mummy anywhere!

"This is a small museum!" the chief said grimly. "The contents must have been stolen from many owners."

Joe pointed to the golden statuettes. "Those belong to the Egyptian Museum in New York. Ali stole them. We were commissioned by Curator Henry Wilcox to find them."

"We will see that Wilcox gets them back," the chief promised. "But first, all these things will have to be listed by a professional Egyptologist. I will phone for Mahmoud Salim at the museum."

Salim arrived an hour later. He identified the mummy in the pickup as one that had disappeared from a dig conducted some time ago. Taking out a notebook, he inspected Kemal's collection and listed the pieces.

The professor finally broke down and confessed that for years he had been buying stolen Egyptian artifacts.

"We will take this gang to jail," the chief declared. "We have all the evidence we need to build a case against them."

While his officers handcuffed the prisoners, he turned to Frank and Joe. "You have done a great service to my country, and I wish to thank you for your excellent detective work," he said with a grateful smile.

But Frank looked glum. "Trouble is, we did not quite accomplish what we set out to do."

"What is that?" the chief asked curiously.

"Find the missing mummy!"

20

Kidnapped in New York

The chief questioned Kemal, but the professor re-
fused to reveal where the mummy was. Finally the
prisoners were taken to the squad cars for transpor-
tation to the Caîro prison. The chief dropped the
Hardys off at the museum, where they reported the
capture of the thieves and the recovery of the stolen
artifacts.

The curator was shocked to hear that Professor
Kemal was the customer of the gang. "One of my
trusted staff members!" he wailed. "I just cannot
believe it!"

"Would you mind if we called New York?" Frank
asked. "I'd like to tell Mr. Wilcox about the result of
our search."

"Please," the curator offered and nervously handed Frank the telephone. "He will be very upset about the missing mummy!"

It turned out that Wilcox was not in, so Frank spoke to William Colden. Colden commended the boys on finding the stolen statuettes. "Sam Radley had no success with his investigation," he said. "No wonder. The thieves were in Egypt."

He paused for a moment, then went on, "But how could you possibly lose the mummy? That's what we sent you to Cairo for. You'd better stay and find it!"

"I have a hunch it isn't here," Frank said. "We'd like to return to New York and follow a lead."

There was another pause. Then Colden said, "When are you coming in?"

"We'll try to get seats on the next flight," Frank replied.

After he hung up, Joe looked at him questioningly. "What lead in New York were you talking about?"

"I just had a hunch, and I could kick myself for not thinking of it sooner!"

"What?"

"The mummy may have never left New York!"

Joe stared at him, then slapped his forehead with the palm of his right hand. "Of course! We may have been guarding an empty casket all along!"

"Norma was still at the museum when we went to

Bayport before our trip," Frank continued. "Perhaps she managed to remove the mummy just before the case was sealed!"

After picking up their bags from the Nile–Hilton Hotel, the Hardys took a taxi to the airport. They were lucky to get two seats on a flight that was leaving only an hour later and would arrive in New York late that afternoon.

"It's really much longer than it seems," Joe said with a grin, "because of the time difference."

"That's all right with me," Frank said. "I'm so tired I'll sleep all the way to New York."

They arrived at Kennedy Airport relatively rested, even though they were somewhat stiff from the long trip in cramped quarters. After they had cleared their luggage through customs, they heard an announcemen over the loudspeaker.

"Frank and Joe Hardy, please report to the information desk!"

A man was waiting for them. "I'm Stan Jelke," he introduced himself. "Mr. Wilcox sent me. I have a car waiting outside."

"Great!" Frank said. "It'll save us catching a taxi."

Jelke ushered them into the back seat of a green sedan and slammed the door. Then he climbed behind the wheel and started the car. A glass partition separated him from the Hardys in the rear.

Frank and Joe, preoccupied with the problem of

finding the mummy, took little notice of the ride to Manhattan. Suddenly Joe pointed. "Frank! We're supposed to go uptown but we're headed for the docks!"

"You're right. I guess this guy got lost. We'd better tell him."

Frank rapped on the glass partition, but the driver paid no attention.

"He must be deaf!" Frank muttered and hammered more loudly on the glass.

The driver looked at him in the rearview mirror and leered threateningly.

Joe tried the door handle on his side. "It's locked!" he cried.

Frank found his door was locked, too. "We're being kidnapped!"

"Can we break through this glass?" Joe asked.

"Let's try."

They were searching along the edge of the glass where it joined the front seat, when the driver pressed a button on the dashboard. Gas seeped into the back seat and almost instantly the Hardys blacked out!

They came to feeling groggy and weak. Breathing deeply to clear their heads, they looked around. They were in a small room covered with dust and cobwebs. Some two-by-fours were stacked on end in one corner, and a number of broken crates lined one wall. The glass in the narrow, barred window was shattered.

The boys pulled themselves to their feet. "Where are we?" Joe asked.

Frank walked to the window and looked out. "Must be a warehouse near the docks," he reported. "Obviously it hasn't been used for years. We're on the top floor."

Joe had tried the door. "And we're locked in," he added.

"My hunch was right," Frank muttered. "Now I'm sure the mummy isn't in Egypt but in New York. And William Colden was the only person who knew we were coming back!"

"The people in Cairo knew it," Joe pointed out. "They could have called someone."

"H'm. But then, Colden was the one who supervised the crating of the mummy case. He's a prime suspect in our case, Joe! But how can we prove it if we don't get out of this dump?"

"I have an idea!" Joe's eyes lighted up. He pulled out of his pocket the emergency kit his father had given him on Rubassa and went to the door. He tried the various miniature tools on the lock, but to no avail. "You think that little explosive capsule would work?" he asked his brother.

"Shove it into the lock as far as you can," Frank advised. "Then we'll hit it with a two-by-four."

Their plan worked. When Frank activated the capsule, there was a tremendous noise and heavy smoke enveloped the room. But the door had burst open!

Holding their noses, the young detectives stumbled out of their prison. They ran down the stairs, gasping and coughing, then stopped on the landing for a moment to recover.

Finally Frank said, "Let's get a cab and go straight to the museum!"

When they arrived, they found Mr. Wilcox in his office. He had not sent the car to pick them up. Instantly he called in Najeeb Salim and William Colden and told them what had happened to the Hardy boys.

"Mr. Salim, did you know we were coming back from Egypt today?" Frank questioned the assistant curator.

"No. I had no idea. As a matter of fact, I've just returned to the museum this afternoon. I have been convalescing until today."

"And you were in the hospital when the mummy was prepared for the trip," Joe added.

Salim nodded. "Of course. You took me there yourself."

"But Mr. Colden supervised the crating, and *he* knew we were coming into Kennedy Airport," Frank said slowly.

Colden stared at him. "So? What are you trying to say?"

"That you removed the mummy before we took the coffin aboard the *Admiral Halsey!*"

Colden turned ashen white. Then he snarled. "You're crazy! The Egyptian sun must have been too much for you!"

"You wanted to create the impression that the pharaoh had been removed aboard ship," Frank continued. "You, Ali, and Norma Jones didn't want Mr. Salim, or *anyone*, to accompany the empty crate to Egypt. And Norma served you only half a cup of coffee so it would look as if you and Mr. Salim had both drunk the poison. But when you realized we were going to escort the mummy, Ali and Londy were told to do everything possible to make us think it had been stolen on board."

Colden jumped up from his seat. "This is utterly ridiculous!" he screamed. "Mr. Wilcox, how can you sit there and have these young whippersnappers accuse me?"

"Aren't you wondering why you haven't heard from your friends in Cairo?" Joe put in before Wilcox had a chance to comment. "It's because Fuad Kemal, Ahmed Ali, Butch Londy, and Norma Jones are in jail, together with the rest of the gang!"

"And aren't you wondering if they talked?" Frank prodded.

Colden covered his face with his hands while Wilcox and Salim stared in surprise. Finally the curator regained his composure. "I'd better call the police," he said, his voice shaking.

Two officers arrived and Wilcox gave them permission to search Colden's office for clues. Frank and Joe joined one of them, while the other remained to guard Colden.

The group searched the assistant curator's desk, his files, and his telephone directory for clues. Frank opened the closet. It was quite large, and he went inside. Pushing aside some lab coats and Colden's jacket, he began to examine closely the top shelf, the walls, and the floor. One of the wooden floorboards appeared to be loose at one end. He lifted it and found that the adjoining boards came up, too. Excited, Frank removed them and found an oblong box, about five feet in length, underneath.

"Joe!" he cried out. "Come here, quick!"

The boys stared at the box for a moment, then took it out and put it on the rug in the office. They removed the lid and shouted with joy.

In the box lay the missing mummy!

It was swathed from head to foot in the tightly bound linen they remembered so well, and the two artificial eyes gleamed through the holes in the bandage.

"You were right, Frank!" Joe said. "Our mummy

never left this museum! It's been here all along—just waiting to be sold by Colden. Come on, let's show it to Mr. Wilcox!"

When the curator saw the box, he looked at it in awe. "This is incredible!" he finally murmured.

"You boys did a wonderful job," Najeeb Salim said admiringly. "I'm happy you were on hand when I was poisoned. And," he added with a weak smile, "I'm glad not to be under suspicion any longer!"

Frank and Joe were glad, too. Yet, the same thought went through both their minds. Would they ever be called on another case? They had no idea that soon they would be working on the *Mystery of Smugglers Cove.*

Just then the telephone rang. It was Colden's secretary. "A Mr. Stan Jelke is waiting in his car downstairs for Mr. Colden," she told Wilcox, who had answered the call. "He said Mr. Colden was to be ready for him, but I know he's in your office—"

"Bill will be right down," Wilcox replied. "Tell Jelke to wait." He hung up and turned to his assistant, who had already been handcuffed. "Who's Stan Jelke?"

Frank spoke up. "He's the chauffeur Colden sent to take us to the warehouse!"

"We'll arrest him downstairs," the police officer in charge said. "Come along, Mr. Colden."

Colden stood up and shrugged. "I tried my best

to frighten you Hardys off the case," he muttered. "What did I do wrong?"

"You wouldn't listen to the pharaoh's warning," Frank replied. "He was trying to tell you that crime doesn't pay."

You are invited to join

THE OFFICIAL HARDY BOYS™ FAN CLUB!

Be the first in your neighborhood to find out about Frank and Joe's newest adventures in the *Hardy Boys™ Mystery Reporter,* and to receive your official membership card. Just send your name, age, address, and zip code to:

The Official Hardy Boys™ Fan Club
Wanderer Books
1230 Avenue of the Americas
New York, NY 10020

Don't Miss

THE HARDY BOYS™ MYSTERY STORIES
by Franklin W. Dixon

NANCY DREW MYSTERY STORIES®
by Carolyn Keene

Plus exciting survival stories in

The Hardy Boys™ Handbook
Seven Stories of Survival
by Franklin W. Dixon with Sheila Link

And solve-it-yourself mysteries

The Hardy Boys™ Who-Dunnit Book
by Franklin W. Dixon

Nancy Drew® Book of Hidden Clues
by Carolyn Keene